THE HEART'S LONGING

Rosie, a young widow, lived alone with her six-year-old son, Andy, in a small village in South Africa. She was about to open a small antiques shop when handsome Josh McGregor, who was blind, came into her life. Rosie knew that Andy would love a dad like Josh, but would the secret she harboured always come between her and any chance of happiness with him? Would she ever have a future if she refused to face up to her past?

Books by Beverley Winter
in the Linford Romance Library:

BEVERLEY WINTER

THE HEART'S LONGING

Complete and Unabridged

LINFORD
Leicester

First published in Great Britain in 2002

First Linford Edition
published 2004

British Library CIP Data

Winter, Beverley
    The heart's longing.—Large print ed.—
Linford romance library
    1. Love stories
    2. Large type books
    I. Title
    823.9′14 [F]

    ISBN 1–84395–269–6

Published by
F. A. Thorpe (Publishing)
Anstey, Leicestershire

Set by Words & Graphics Ltd.
Anstey, Leicestershire
Printed and bound in Great Britain by
T. J. International Ltd., Padstow, Cornwall

This book is printed on acid-free paper

1

Josh McGregor's dark eyes narrowed in shocked disbelief as he stared at the newspaper, a week-old copy of the Sunday Crier he'd discovered in the crew room which was situated at one end of the aircraft hangar. He tossed the tabloid to one side, wishing he'd never laid eyes on it. The caption beneath the photograph was like a body blow.

The engagement is announced between . . .

The words recurred in his stunned mind like a car on a race track, round and round and round, but being a thorough, meticulous man by nature, he retrieved the newspaper and forced himself to read the article again, his gaze lingering on the smiling face of the woman in the photograph. The sheer shock of seeing those large blue eyes gazing adoringly into those of another man had left him reeling, not least because the man in question was a colleague and trusted aide.

Josh felt as though the kick-boxer in his stomach had just returned with a vengeance, causing the breath to leave his chest. His lips twisted in self-mockery. Little wonder she'd been taking such pains to avoid him of late. Gina Huntley, South Africa's super-model, had been 'too busy' planning matrimony to his best friend, Lieutenant Geoff Pearson.

He felt a strange, despairing sense of déjà vu. It wasn't the first time a woman had cheated on him. His wife, Lucinda, had run off six years previously with an American airman.

'Ready, Major?'

The voice of Captain Ross broke into his thoughts.

Josh exerted an iron discipline over his churning emotions. He thrust aside the hurt and anger which threatened to overwhelm him and gathered up his equipment. He could not afford a lapse in concentration just as he was trying out a new manoeuvre. Determined to carry on with his self-imposed mission, he turned and gave a thumbs-up sign to the pilot of the small aircraft which would carry him up to twelve thousand feet above the earth for his next jump.

Sky-diving was a sport which had always fascinated him. Second only to flying, it was the love of his life. As a commissioned officer in the South African Air Force, he was in the fortunate position of being able to indulge his hobby, making jumps as often as he pleased, like now, while he was technically on leave from the Air Force base in Pretoria. If this manoeuvre worked, he intended to pass on the technique to a colleague who was always looking for new training methods.

Josh's expression was grim as the aircraft climbed high over the red sands of the Kalahari Desert. It was strange territory but at least he could expect a soft landing in the porous, sandy soil. In superb physical condition, Josh knew he was ready for anything. Not that he expected any difficulties, of course. He'd been over the technique a dozen times in his head.

He tumbled out of the plane and began the initial free-fall, floating down silently and enjoying the usual blast of wind against his face. An experienced parachutist, he never failed to appreciate the adrenaline rush as he jumped from the aircraft.

It was an automatic reflex to position his body correctly, but even as his body co-operated with the correct principle of aerodynamics, his mind veered dangerously off course. To his way of thinking, the betrayal of his colleague was an even greater insult than that of his girlfriend, Gina. Women were notoriously fickle. Hadn't that been his experience? But his buddy, Geoff, of all people!

The unwelcome realisation surfaced that the affair had probably been going on for months under his very nose. He and Geoff had worked together day in and day out. How his friend must have laughed behind his back! Like a missile appearing from nowhere, Josh's fury suddenly erupted. It ripped through his defences and exploded inside him like a destructive agent of death, depriving him of all sense of reason, time and space.

It was then that the manoeuvre went pear-shaped. Too late, Josh realised that he had missed his cue. He had left the attempted move too late. He was already too close to the ground!

Not a man given to panic, he quickly reassessed the situation and moved to check his fall, but a further complication arose when he became inextricably caught up in his canopy, something which had never happened to him before. Cursing himself for his carelessness, he decided there was nothing for it but to turn around in order to approach the drop zone from a different angle.

It had been an unpardonable lapse and he knew it.

Swiftly he tried to bring himself upright once more, while in the horizontal position, only to become further entangled in the ropes. To crown his misfortunes, the reserve 'chute failed to function.

From five hundred feet in the air, Josh realised he was falling towards the ground at seventy miles an hour. A man who was unaccustomed to fear, he told himself that this couldn't be happening. He was no amateur, he was an experienced sky diver, for pity's sake!

Because he was travelling horizontally he was going much faster. He was soon going to hit the ground!

An icy calm settled over him. He braved himself for landing, and as the unwelcome red dust of the Kalahari rose to choke him, he thought unemotionally that there wasn't even time for a dying wish . . .

★   ★   ★

It was a still, crisp morning. Autumn had arrived with its palette of gold, russet, copper and flaming scarlet, and every detail of the landscape was faithfully reflected in the glassy waters of the dam. It was the kind of perfection which had inspired many a celebrated artist to produce his finest work, yet it did nothing for Josh McGregor. He lived in a world of grey.

His prognosis, he reflected morosely, appeared to be somewhat grey. A man not usually given to self pity, he was annoyed to find that his whole outlook of late had become grey, and his thoughts on this particular morning were certainly grey!

'Dan!' he roared, making no effort to curb his frustration.

A muddy yellow Labrador left off snuffling in the reeds at the edge of the water and bounded towards him. The dog nudged his good leg and gave a soft whine.

'Where the dickens have you been?'

7

Josh demanded irritably. 'It's time to go back.'

The bright, early sun glinted on his dark hair. Now longer than he had worn it while on active service, it was still well-groomed. The sun gilded the expanse of grass alongside the path but did little to illuminate Josh's world or brighten his mood, for he saw only in shapes and outlines. It was as though a grey mantle had descended upon his universe.

Painstakingly, he and Dan negotiated the well-worn track to the cottage some two hundred metres from the water's edge. A small, thatched building, it had been in his family for generations, used as a hideaway for fishing and hiking because of its proximity to the scenic Drakensberg Mountains whose dark, serrated peaks reared dragon-like in the distance.

The area was isolated except for one or two similar holiday dwellings dotted amongst the trees, most of them uninhabited at this time of the year, their owners having long since departed to their homes in time for the start of the new school year. It was the perfect place for a long recuperation.

'Breakfast,' Josh muttered to himself, placing one hand on the porch railing in order to anchor himself more securely as he negotiated the steps.

He wondered if the simple task of frying an egg would produce as much frustration as it had yesterday, when he'd miscalculated the distance between egg and pan and made an unholy mess of the cooker. His jaw hardened in defiance. He would teach himself to do all the normal things again, even if it killed him!

'Steak and eggs,' he informed Dan as he limped into the kitchen.

Dan made a sound in his throat which could have been sympathetic agreement. Steak and eggs sounded just fine to him. In fact, everything was just fine now that the master stayed at home all day and that awful woman had disappeared — the one who'd pretended to like him and then kicked him when the master wasn't looking.

Josh felt his way around the tiny kitchen, well used to the position of the fitments and appliances. He opened the fridge and extracted two eggs, determined to get it right this time, hopefully. While he found the steak, his thoughts returned to the near-death experience he'd endured in the Kalahari Desert. He'd been airlifted to a military hospital only to hover for weeks in a purposeless vacuum, his body mangled, his mind numb and his career in shreds. As soon as he'd been discharged he'd taken his younger brother's advice and escaped to the holiday cottage to lick his wounds, and wait for the complete return of his eyesight.

Holding his frustration in check he reached for the frying pan which Agnes always kept in a cupboard under the sink. Agnes was the cleaning woman who came twice weekly from the nearby settlement to flick the duster, wield the vacuum cleaner and deliver one dozen eggs. When he needed other fresh supplies, he and Dan trudged the two slow miles into the village of Winterberg to the small, overpriced supermarket where they made their purchases with the help of the kindly owner, Mrs Du Preez.

Afterwards they would linger on the terrace of the Mountain View Hotel for a long, cool drink before trudging all the way home again. By now Josh was a well-known figure in the village with his yellow dog, his red baseball cap and his white stick.

The aroma of frying steak mingled with that of coffee percolating on the stove. Josh reached into the enamelled bin for the sliced bread, carefully inserted two pieces into the toaster and felt around in the refrigerator for a tub of butter.

'We're going into the village today, Dan,' he growled, 'and don't say that we went two days ago because I know that we did! Truth is, I'll go barking mad — no offence intended, old man — if I have to spend another day sitting around here thinking about frogs and toads.'

Dan thumped his tail. Who was he to argue with the master when it was patently obvious that he had one of his moods coming on? He might not be a trained guide dog exactly, but he knew when the master was unhappy. Besides, they'd been together for a long time.

As he demolished his breakfast, Josh flipped on the television set. He couldn't view the pictures properly but at least he could listen to the news. It helped him to feel there was still a world out there. After a few mouthfuls he was compelled to get up and turn it off again.

'Same old stuff,' he told Dan in disgust. 'Nothing but doom and gloom.'

He had enough of that kind of thing in his life as it was. Josh located the handle of the percolator and carefully poured himself a mug of strong black coffee before limping back to his chair.

He tried not to think of his injuries which, according to the Air Force medics, would heal in due course. All he needed was to build up stamina, keep the muscles exercised and try to think positively about the future, easier said than done when it was patently obvious that his career as he'd known it was finished.

Today his stupid leg was playing up again, and what's more, that familiar ache at the base of his spine had returned. If all that wasn't enough, there was this unspeakable concrete block sitting on his head, and it weighed a ton. Josh drained his mug and slammed it down on the worktop. He very much feared it was going to be another one of those days.

Stubbornly unwilling to abandon the outing, he set off along the road with Dan securely fastened to a lead. Thankfully it was still early enough for the road to be fairly quiet. He could barely see where the road ended and the bush began, but at least he could

13

smell the dank riverbed vegetation to one side, and hear the bubble of the small stream as it dashed over the rocks and emptied itself into the dam beside the cottage.

Despite his present difficulties, Josh considered himself lucky even to be alive. He walked slowly, breathing carefully and making a valiant effort to ignore the pain. To distract himself he fell to thinking about those frogs and toads. There were a dozen or more species in the area and their noisy presence at night often disturbed what little sleep he was able to have. He had learned to distinguish their calls, realising that they were as much part of the night sounds as the insects, the nightjars and the numerous small rodents rustling in the grasses beneath his window.

Josh allowed himself a small, rueful grin. Six months ago, he'd had no interest whatever in frogs, toads and nightjars! He'd had no interest in anything but his work. Then the grin disappeared. What was the saying? All work and no play made Jack a dull boy. Paraphrased, it might read like this, workaholics who indulge their obsessions and neglect their women should not be surprised when said women make other arrangements!

In retrospect, he could see that he hadn't been quite fair to either his ex-wife or his ex-girlfriend! He'd fobbed Gina off whenever talk of an engagement arose. There was always some project or other he'd needed to complete first. Put quite simply, his career had been his true love.

Josh had been popular, disciplined, ambitious and hard working, all the qualities needed for a rapid rise up the military ladder. He'd revelled in his flying and applied himself diligently to his administrative work, directing the numerous personnel under him with skill and flair. Without conceit he knew that he was good. His career prospects had been excellent, until that fateful jump which had changed everything.

'Easy, Dan,' Josh ordered, and as he shortened the lead in his right hand, he grimaced at the sharp pain in his shoulder muscles. 'Hold on a moment, boy,' he gasped.

His hip was nagging unpleasantly and he realised that he would be forced to stop and rest. The injured leg, still not fully operational, was rapidly turning to jelly. As for his semi-blindness, it was now a frustrating fact of life.

'Purely psychological . . . post accident trauma . . . no actual damage to the optic nerve,' the medics had said. 'Take some time out.'

So he'd taken time out, and it was driving him mad. To a man with his personality, six months seemed a long time to remain idle, and he was not a patient person at the best of times. Josh thrust his walking-stick to the left in order to locate the thick, roadside foliage which normally brushed against his legs. He was perplexed to find that it wasn't there.

'Dan, this way,' he ordered sharply, yanking the lead sideways.

Darned dog had pulled him off course! No doubt Dan had caught the scent of something on the other side of the road — a hare, perhaps. Then, without warning, a vehicle erupted out of nowhere, and Josh's head snapped up in alarm.

The car, a blue saloon, crested the rise behind him with a violent squealing of brakes before swerving to avoid him, unsuccessfully. One front wheel clipped Josh roughly on his good leg while the other wheel spun on the gravel, only to propel the car to the opposite side of the road where it ended up with an outraged if subdued roar.

Josh gasped in pain, spun about on the injured leg and hit the Tarmac with a resounding splat. Pain speared him like a hot arrow and blood began oozing from a lip which, he was quite certain, resembled a peeled tomato. Josh emitted a string of creative phrases which only an airman could come up with! There was a moment's appalled silence before the rising tones of an irate female voice sounded in Josh's ears.

'What do you think you're doing, wandering about in the middle of the road like a maniac? Are you blind or something?'

Josh felt for a handkerchief, calmly applied it to the graze on his mouth and schooled his face into an expressionless mask.

'Yes.'

'Yes, you're blind, or yes, you're a maniac?' the voice demanded.

His jaw tightened.

'I happen to be partially sighted.'

He heard an incredulous gasp.

'You're . . . you're really blind? Oh, heavens! Oh, good grief!'

The car door was thrown open as the owner of the voice jumped out with speed, leaving the engine growling.

'I didn't realise. I'm most awfully sorry about this. Are you all right?'

She grabbed his arm — the bad one

— and yanked. Josh was hard pressed not to retaliate. With commendable restraint he bit off another string of phrases.

'Look, mister, you really ought not to be . . .'

'Let loose on an unsuspecting world?' he supplied grimly.

'Well, exactly. I mean, in your condition, surely you shouldn't be wandering about on your own. You could get yourself killed.'

The woman let out a sudden squeak.

'What's that? It can't be a properly-trained guide dog, surely? What's the matter with it? It was leading you clean over the road into the bush.'

Josh dabbed at his lip and fervently hoped that it had stopped bleeding. He pocketed his handkerchief and drew himself up to his full height of six feet two inches.

'Allow me to correct you, lady. Dan is not an it, he's a he.'

She sniffed.

'Well, he deserves to have his licence

revoked. No indicator lights, no hand signals, nothing. The thing didn't even look where he was going.'

'I'll have you know that a temporary lapse of concentration on Dan's part doesn't make him a thing, either,' Josh growled. 'Much as I hate to ask it, lady, would you be so kind as to find my walking-stick?'

'Oh, yes, of course.'

She glanced round, bent to retrieve it and thrust it into his hands along with the red baseball cap.

'Um, are you quite sure you're all right? Can I give you a lift? I'm going into the village.'

Coldly Josh declined. Both legs were now aching but he'd be damned if he was going to allow some female to taxi him around like an invalid. Thanks to her, he felt even more wretched than before, if that were possible. He would be forced to return home.

'We just didn't see you, you know,' the woman added by the way of a belated apology, 'until it was almost too late, that is.'

Josh peered in the direction of the vehicle.

'We?'

'Me and my little blue Volkswagen.'

'I see.'

The woman was crazy as well as reckless, attributing human characteristics to a lump of metal.

'No, you don't,' she reminded him, viewing him unhappily from pansy-dark eyes. 'I feel rather badly about all this.'

'No need,' Josh clipped.

He turned around, gave Dan's lead a yank.

'Come on, boy.'

Rosie Carlisle watched him as he disappeared over the hill. She was normally a kind-hearted young woman but on this occasion exasperation overcame pity. The accident hadn't been her fault at all, anyone could see that! How could she have foreseen as she topped the rise that a crazy man and his dog would be roving drunkenly all over the road?

She shook her head wrathfully. If he really was as blind as he claimed, it was all the more reason for him to stay put inside his house, surely? In the interests of public safety, of course. An alarming thought then assailed her. He hadn't been limping before the accident, had he? She must have done him a serious injury.

Hurriedly, Rosie climbed back into her car and executed the fastest three-point turn she'd ever managed. She slammed the gear lever into first and took off over the hill like a drunken rocket, only to be forced into another frantic stop with another hideous screech of tyres on the other side.

Josh started violently and uttered a short, sharp word the likes of which Rosie had never heard before.

'What on earth now?' he grated.

She leaned breathlessly out of the window.

'Are you quite sure you're all right? You're limping.'

Josh's eyes narrowed to slits, partly in

anger and partly in an effort to see what the confounded woman looked like. All he could make out was a fuzzy outline, which may or may not have been a very thick head of dark hair. He rather hoped it was.

'What is it with you, lady?' he demanded. 'You're intent on killing me. Why don't you just get lost? I told you, I'm fine!'

Unconvinced, Rosie continued to peer through the window, and because the man couldn't see her, she indulged in a thorough and leisurely inspection of his person, and some person it was, too! He wasn't bad-looking at all. In fact, he was downright attractive in a rugged sort of way, with strong features, stunning, darkly-lashed grey eyes, a straight nose and a firm, if disapproving mouth.

'Who are you?' she demanded, ignoring his sour expression. 'I haven't seen you around the village before. Do you live nearby?'

Josh's eyebrows rose.

'What's it to you? Now be a good girl and run along. Hasn't your mother told you never to pick up strangers, especially ones who can't see?'

'I'm not a girl. I'm twenty-six, and I wasn't picking you up!'

'Whatever,' Josh said nastily. 'I have no further desire to stand here conversing with a twenty-six-year-old bat out of hell. Good day to you.'

He turned and limped away. Regretfully, Rosie surveyed his departing back. The poor man was dreadfully hung up about being blind, wasn't he? And she hadn't been trying to pick him up, honestly she hadn't. She'd simply been concerned about him. Who wouldn't be?

'Good day to you, too,' she said somewhat childishly before pointing the Volkswagen's nose in the direction of the village.

Josh returned to the cottage in an even worse mood than before. If his head had been pounding ten minutes ago it was nothing compared with how the drums felt now, not to mention that concrete block. He groped his way into the bathroom, found a couple of the strong, painkilling tablets the doctor had given him for special use and flung himself down on the bed. Damned women drivers!

It was three days before he felt able to attempt another walk into the village. Despite the warm sunshine there was a chilly autumn wind soughing through the foliage. He inhaled deeply. Dan, only too happy to be having another outing, was pulling hard at the lead.

'Easy, Dan,' Josh cautioned.

At the end of the lane, Dan turned left in a confident manner as he accompanied the master along the by now familiar road.

'Too much of the world,' Josh informed his dog as they trudged down the road, 'is run on the theory that you don't need road manners if you're a five-ton truck or a small blue Volkswagen!'

To keep from boredom, he fell to

thinking about small blue Volkswagens and the women who drove them. He'd never admit it to a soul, but he'd have given anything to have been able to see the racing driver's face!

'With any luck, Dan,' he informed the dog confidently, 'we'll be quite safe today. We'll not run into that confounded woman again.'

2

Rosie Carlisle screeched into the small parking area of the Mountain View Hotel, flung herself out of the blue Volkswagen and dashed inside for her shift. She hated to be late, but Andy had taken his time over his breakfast and then hadn't been able to find his school shoes.

In the small ante-room reserved for the staff, she placed her handbag in an empty locker and deftly tied a frilly white apron around her trim waist.

'Sorry I'm late,' she panted as she rushed into the office.

Her twin sister, Lucy Allbright, sat frowning over a spreadsheet.

'That's all right, love,' she replied vaguely as she continued to study the computer screen. 'How have things been with you?'

27

'Well, I managed to get that consignment unpacked last night, you know, the stuff I bought in Johannesburg last week. I'm almost ready to open my business. And did I tell you that I'm painting the flat above the shop? I'm delighted with it. It's quite roomy. I'll have to start looking around for a small sofa and one or two other bits of furniture, oh, and a couple of beds.'

Her sister looked up sharply.

'You don't have any beds? Why didn't you say so, Rosie? I could have let you have two from the hotel. We've a couple in storage. Don't tell me you've been sleeping on the floor.'

'Well, yes, on a pile of duvets, actually. I told Andy we could pretend to be camping in the mountains.'

Lucy grinned.

'Your son will make a fine game ranger some day, never fear. He's mad about anything which breathes and wears fur. Any other news?'

'Well, if you call near-homicide news, then wait for it,' Rosie announced dramatically. 'I practically ran some-body over on Monday.'

'You what?' Lucy exclaimed.

'I nearly killed an idiot,' Rosie repeated, adding for effect, 'a blind one.'

Her sister blinked.

'Who? Where?'

'About two miles out of the village. I've no idea who he is but he looked as though he'd had the fright of his life, but it was all his own fault.'

She gave a slow smile.

'He wasn't half bad looking, either. The proverbial tall, dark and hand-some. Oh, and he had an awful yellow dog, and a white stick, a red baseball cap.'

'Oh, you mean Josh McGregor?' Lucy interrupted in dismay. 'The poor man! You'll have to drive more carefully in future, Rosie.'

Rosie snorted.

'It wasn't my fault! The moron was making like a tipsy crab, wandering sideways all over the road. He ought to have known better.'

'You didn't hurt him, did you?'

Rosie flushed guiltily.

'No, of course not. At least, he said he was OK.'

Lucy studied her sister thoughtfully.

'That's all right, then. He's one of our best patrons, you know, and we wouldn't like to see him upset. He's been through a lot recently, or so I hear. The village grapevine is as active as ever, my dear. Aren't you glad you've come to live amongst us?'

'Not with maniacs like him around! But I wouldn't mention the incident to anyone if I were you. I don't want it blown up out of all proportion.'

'Quite. Small things do tend to assume almighty proportions. It's called the village mentality. However, villages do have their good points, too, you know. People care about one another. Of course, there's a fine line between caring and interfering.'

'Exactly!' Rosie continued. 'The nice thing about living in a village is that even when you don't know what you're doing, someone else always does.'

'Take heart, Rosie. You'll soon get back into our quaint, little ways.'

Lucy heaved herself up out of her chair.

'Thanks for coming in today.'

'No problem. Where would you like me to start? Andy is going straight to a friend's to play after school, so seeing I'm here until four o'clock, you might as well make good use of me.'

'I will,' her sister told her gratefully. 'I really appreciate you giving up your time, Rosie, just when you're so busy yourself. We're a bit short staffed, as I told you, with two waitresses away and the assistant chef down with the flu. Would you take the terrace until midday? We usually get one or two customers before lunch. Then you can help my poor, overworked Daniel in the kitchen.'

'Sure,' Rosie replied as she bustled off to wipe the tables.

To be honest, she had been planning

31

on doing a little dusting and cataloguing in her shop today, but when Lucy had telephoned earlier sounding desperate, she hadn't liked to disappoint her. Lucy and Daniel worked hard and deserved all the help they could get. Besides, her sister was in the eighth month of a difficult and long-awaited pregnancy.

The marble-topped tables and padded wrought-iron chairs were pristine by the time Rosie had finished with her spray bottle and duster. She adjusted the sun umbrellas, replaced the ash trays and then swept the paving which bordered the lawn. As there were no customers as yet, she took herself inside to polish the glasses, determined to keep a sharp lookout through the dining-room window in case anyone arrived.

Lucy waddled through with a fresh pile of table napkins.

'Ah. There's someone out there now. Will you see to him, please, Rosie?'

Rosie replaced the glass she was

cleaning and sailed out to the terrace with a smile on her face. She was feeling happy today, and it would be fun to help out. It was such a glorious day, too.

The first thing she saw was the dog. Rosie's smile disappeared. She was afraid of big dogs, and this one was glaring at her like she was a horned toad, or something! Perhaps he thought she'd tried to finish him off along with his master the other day, and was just getting ready to take his vengeance.

Rosie approached the table gingerly, keeping an apprehensive eye on the Labrador. So far, so good. She even relaxed a little when she noticed he seemed to have lost interest in her and was yawning his head off. Rosie turned her attention to the man sitting at the table.

'Good morning, sir,' she sang. 'Isn't it a lovely day? May I take your order, please?'

Josh McGregor started. He glanced up in appalled disbelief. Surely it couldn't be that woman again! He narrowed his gaze in order to see more clearly; a futile effort, for despite the brightness of the sunshine, all he could make out was the outline of Rosie's hair. Slowly he concentrated his gaze on her body, and was just able to discern that it curved in all the right places. Yes, it was the same woman all right. He scowled.

'You have a knack of turning up to ruin my day, don't you? What will it be this time, arsenic in the orange juice?'

Rosie ignored the jibe. The man had no social graces whatever!

She announced brightly, 'In addition to orange juice we have fresh lemonade as well as all the usual carbonated drinks. Or would you prefer tea or coffee, sir? Perhaps you'd like a cream scone with your coffee.'

'Spare me the sales patter,' Josh interrupted irritably. 'Coffee will do.'

'Certainly, sir. Coming right up.'

The man might have a thorn under his paw but he needn't think he could spoil her day, Rosie decided. She had no use for people who moped about like dyspeptic morons.

While Rosie was preparing the coffee the kind-hearted side of her nature surfaced. The man was obviously unhappy. It couldn't be easy to be blind. A few minutes later she reappeared with a tray laden with two cups, a silver coffee pot, a plate of Lucy's home-made scones, butter and various small pots of jam.

'Love is like a butterfly,' she sang softly as she set the tray on the table.

Her voice might not be anywhere near as good as Dolly Parton's but at least she could sing in tune, and everyone ought to be singing on such a lovely morning!

Josh pursed his lips. There was nothing worse than a determinedly cheerful individual spreading sweetness and light when he had no wish to be sweetened or lightened. All he wanted was a cup of coffee, for crying out loud! He heard her chair scrape on the paving and listened in disbelief at the sound of the liquid sloshing into his cup.

'There is no need to play nursemaid and pour my coffee,' he snapped. 'I can manage.'

'I'm sure you can, sir,' Rosie said soothingly. 'It's just that I'm pouring my own, so I might as well pour yours at the same time. Milk?'

She waved the jug in the air. Josh couldn't believe his ears.

'Pouring your own? I do not recollect that I invited you to join me.'

He glared in her direction, looking very large, very cross and very menacing; a fighting man in every sense of the word, but Rosie refused to be intimidated.

'Milk?' she repeated.

'Oh, go away!'

She set his cup down on the table before him, took a deep breath and informed him calmly, 'I'm not going anywhere, sir, I'll leave your coffee black, then. There's nothing worse than milk in something when you don't like it.'

Josh blinked incredulously. The woman really meant to stay!

'You are a very forward young woman,' he told her furiously.

Rosie grinned.

'Not really. It's my coffee break and I've decided to have it out here in the sunshine. The view's heavenly, all those mountains in the distance, looking very dark and dragon-like. That's why they're called the Drakensberg, isn't it? From the Dutch, meaning dragon mountains. Such an apt description, I always think.'

She peeped at him from beneath her lashes.

'Perhaps you'd like to try a scone? They're home-made.' She added proudly, 'By my twin sister, you know. She does most of the baking here.'

She reached for a scone and buttered it.

'Apricot or strawberry?'

'I didn't order scones,' Josh growled,

feeling thoroughly exasperated.

Couldn't a man have any privacy in this place? Furthermore, the blasted woman seemed unable to stop gabbling.

'No, sir, you didn't,' Rosie agreed sweetly, 'but I reckoned you could use a little sugar this morning.'

Ignoring his look of outrage, she repeated, 'Apricot or strawberry? If neither is to your liking I can always fetch the honey.'

'Oh, for crying in a bucket,' Josh burst out, 'I'll have the apricot!'

Rosie gave a small, satisfied smile.

'Certainly, sir.'

Looking thunderous, Josh reached for his coffee, located the handle and drained his cup. Rosie immediately topped it up again. She spread a scone with apricot jam, placed a large dollop of cream in the centre and passed him the plate.

'There you are, sir.'

'Thank you,' Josh said curtly.

'You're welcome, sir.'

He choked on his first bite then when he had regained his breath he thundered, 'I would appreciate it if you didn't address me as 'sir' in that ingratiating manner. It's profoundly irritating. It reminds me . . . '

He snapped his mouth shut. Rosie stared at him with interest.

'Of what?'

He hesitated, a bleakness in his eyes.

'It reminds me of my work.'

'Oh? In what way?' Rosie persisted, knowing it wasn't her business.

The trouble was, the man was beginning to fascinate her.

'I was in the Air Force.'

Her eyes widened.

'You were in the military? What rank?'

Josh hesitated. He had no intention of baring his all to this nosey female, but speaking about his career was a peculiar relief.

'Major,' he clipped.

Rosie was impressed. He was young to be a Major.

'My husband was in the South African Defence Force, too,' she remarked matter-of-factly.

'Was?'

'He died in action while fighting terrorists in Angola.'

Josh's head jerked up. He tried to read her expression and gave up.

'I'm sorry,' he said quietly.

'Oh, it was a long time ago. Life goes on, doesn't it?'

Deliberately, Rosie injected brightness into her voice.

'Perhaps not in quite the same way as before, but it goes on nevertheless, with fresh challenges all along the way.'

She stood up and began collecting the crockery.

'My coffee break is up and I must get back to work. Goodbye, Major.'

He lifted a hand.

'You'll bring me the bill.'

It was an order rather than a question.

'Oh, no, not at all. It was on the house today.'

40

Josh looked as though she'd slapped him.

'I don't need your charity,' he retorted coldly, 'any more than I need your pity. You'll bring me that bill.'

Rosie viewed him thoughtfully.

'Just as you wish, but it wasn't meant to be charity, you know, just a gesture of friendship. And I wouldn't pity a great hunk of meat like you if you paid me. I've enough problems of my own. Besides, you're big enough and ugly enough to take care of yourself.'

Before she could stop it, her unruly tongue ran on.

'Besides, I'll have you know that for some unknown and very annoying reason you're the best-looking male specimen I've ever laid eyes on. It's like you have this blatant and very masculine aura. I daresay you have all the women in creation falling over you. No, it's not pity I feel, Major, it's plain attraction. There! I've said it. And I don't know what's come over me. I'm a very shy girl, normally.'

A dull tide of red had appeared above the collar of Josh's blue polo shirt.

'I see. In that case I . . . er . . . accept your coffee. Thank you.'

'My pleasure.'

Hastily Rosie picked up the tray.

'Wait.'

'Yes?'

'Your hair,' he muttered, 'what colour is it?'

Rosie's pink mouth dropped open.

'My hair? It's black, long and thick. It's the bane of my life.'

Major McGregor nodded.

'I thought so. Goodbye, Ms . . . er . . . '

'Carlisle. Rosie Carlisle,' she supplied, and scuttled inside.

'Oh, heavenly saints,' she groaned as she loaded the crockery into the dishwasher. 'I'm out of my mind! Why can't I control my tongue?'

What had come over her, saying all those things to a perfect stranger? He must think she was a man-hungry, little widow on the make — or an absolute nutcase.

At the end of her shift Rosie said goodbye to Lucy, retrieved her handbag from the locker and raced off to collect Andy from Tommy Mitchell's house.

'What's for dinner, Mum?' her small son demanded as they climbed the concrete stairway to the little flat above the shop.

His face was grubby and his short dark hair stood up in spikes.

Rosie gave an inward sigh as she tried to focus on food. There hadn't been much money left over after she'd poured her meagre savings into the deposit needed for renting the shop. The only reason the agent had let her have it was because she'd been prepared to take the flat above as well, despite the fact that it needed considerable renovations. There certainly wasn't much left over for furnishing and decoration. As it was, it would be a struggle to feed them for the first month at least.

'Spaghetti bolognaise,' she told him.

'But we had that last night.'

'Yes, I know. We're having the left-overs tonight, with custard for afters.'

'Gee, Mum, you ought to learn how to cook a few more things,' Andy told his mother with childish candour. 'A man's got to eat around here.'

Rosie ruffled his hair before fishing in her copious bag for the door key.

'Tomorrow night, we'll have meat-balls, OK?'

Andy brightened.

'OK.'

'Now go and take a bath while I set the table. We'll tackle your homework after we've eaten.'

'Aw, Mum. Can't I watch my wildlife video instead?'

She assumed her non-negotiable voice.

'No way! It's bath, supper, and then homework. Tomorrow's Friday and there'll be no homework. You can watch it then.'

Andy sighed heavily. It had been a nice try. He took his sturdy, six-year-old body off to the bathroom and flung his black plastic spider, his green rubber snake and his yellow bath sponge into the swirling water. Mothers were so boring! Thoughtfully he picked up the sponge and squeezed it. He wished he had a father, a big, tall one like Tommy Mitchell's.

By Friday morning, Rosie was ready to do business. She walked Andy to the village school and returned to the flat to do the dishes and make the beds. Just before nine o'clock she went downstairs with her purse and emptied its contents into the till. She had to have some sort of a float so that she could give people change, but all she could come up with was very little, which was, in fact, her lifeline until the end of next week. Rosie slammed the till shut, consoling herself with the thought that her natural optimism and ability to work hard would soon result in the business building into something really profitable.

Not that she knew a great deal about antiques, but she was a fast learner, and she'd been poring over books on the subject all year. Besides, collecting Victoriana had always been a hobby of hers, so it had seemed natural to arrange her collection on the shelves, add to it here and there from catalogues and private house sales, and then set up in business as Rosie's Treasures. At least she was her own boss, and able to be on hand for Andy.

Recently, some of her finds had been wonderful, the genuine article! But mostly she sold authentic replicas based on actual period designs. Before the year was out, Rosie hoped to build up her collection of jewellery and silverware, and in December she had plans to make an impressive window display entitled A Victorian Christmas. Her head was buzzing with all the festive centrepieces, red velvet Christmas dolls, tree trims, damask mantle runners and traditional cone wreaths she intended to make during the long, lonely evenings when Andy was asleep. She made a mental note to begin collecting a variety of pine cones and pretty ribbons as soon as she could.

The shop bell pinged, intruding into her pleasant thoughts. Rosie spun round to see a plump, grey-haired woman in a brown hat marching determinedly into the middle of the shop. A large, leather handbag was clutched under one arm.

'Good morning,' Rosie greeted her politely. 'May I help you?'

'No thanks, I just came to see what you're up to. You're new to Winterberg, aren't you? Moved into the flat upstairs, I see.'

Rosie hid a smile. The village grapevine was already at work.

'Yes. I'm Rosie Carlisle.'

'I know, dear. You're Lucy Allbright's sister. I'm Maggie Morgan from the big house on the hill. Been here for years. You married, then?'

Rosie hesitated.

'I'm a widow.'

Mrs Morgan leaned forward avidly.

'Are you, now? Any children?'

'Yes, I have a six-year-old son.'

Rosie pretended to rearrange a collection of silver thimbles. There was absolutely no way she would be drawn into discussing Andy. She had no intention of revealing the secret of Andy's origins to anyone. For one thing, if the truth were known, he might be taken away from her. That was something she would not be able to bear. Lucy was the only person who knew, and Lucy was absolutely trustworthy. Lucy would keep her secret. Besides, what little she did tell Mrs Morgan would be all over the village by lunch time!

'Only the one? Me, now, I have two sons,' Mrs Morgan boasted. 'A daughter as well, all married. Tell me, Mrs Carlisle, what is it exactly that you sell in here? Doesn't look like very much to me.'

'Well, no, but it's early days yet,'

Rosie explained, adding, 'I hope to build up the business to something really big in due course.'

Her glance fell on a tray of silver items near the counter.

'Do you sew, Mrs Morgan? May I interest you in this small pair of silver sewing scissors with the pewter case? The case is ornate and finely detailed, as you can see.'

Mrs Morgan peered at it doubtfully.

'The case is cast in pewter following an original Victorian design, you know,' Rosie added encouragingly.

'How much?'

Rosie told her, hoping the price was not too high. It would not do to discourage potential buyers, but at the same time she had to make a profit.

'I'll take it,' Mrs Morgan said. 'It'll make a nice little gift for my daughter, Cecilia. She's always sewing.'

She produced a bulging purse and extracted a large note.

'Thank you, dearie. Keep the change. I'll tell my friend about your shop.'

When she'd gone, Rosie did a little jig. Her first sale! And an excellent one at that, thanks to Mrs Morgan's generosity. Carefully she deposited the note in the till. Andy would have meatballs every night for a week, if he so wished!

Taking exquisite care, Rosie set about dusting the china. There were some wonderful Aubusson patterned cups and saucers with fine gold rims which needed to be displayed more prominently. She completed the task, moving one or two other items until they were arranged to her satisfaction, and stood back to admire the display. The doorbell pinged once more.

'Mrs Carlisle? I'm Etta de Wit. My friend, Maggie, has just bought something from you and I won't be outdone. What can you show me?'

Hiding another smile, Rosie looked around.

'What about one of these silk scarves? They're pure silk, decorated with a chinoiserie design.'

'A what?'

'A design inspired by eighteenth-century wallpapers. See, here's a rather attractive one in deep blue with pink flowers.'

Mrs de Wit beamed.

'Perfect.'

As Rosie wrapped the purchase, Mrs de Wit took it upon herself to relay the village gossip. It was obvious that both Maggie and Etta kept an eagle eye on everyone's affairs.

'That Sam Petty was livid when he heard you'd rented this property,' she remarked. 'Wanted it for himself so he could expand his joinery business. Your garden backs on to his timber yard, you see.'

Rosie rang up the sale, listening with half an ear.

'Hasn't been here that long,' Mrs de Wit was now saying, 'three months or so.' She paused. 'May I call you Rosie? He's disabled, you know.'

Rosie blinked.

'Who's disabled? The joiner?'

'No, dear, the man who's moved into that thatched cottage near the dam. Blind as a bat, they tell me. Walks with a stick, always in the company of a dirty great Labrador bounding about all over the place.'

'Oh, you mean the Major?'

'Major McGregor, yes. You've met him, then? Such a glum-looking individual, isn't he? It's rumoured that he had some sort of an accident in the Forces, but my guess is that it's all a great bluff.'

'A bluff?'

'Certainly. I don't believe he's really blind, not for one moment. It's all a disguise, a cover, and an extremely clever one, at that.'

At Rosie's look of bewilderment Mrs de Wit patiently explained.

'He's a spy, dear.'

'A spy?' Rosie gasped in utter disbelief.

'Yes, dear. One of those awful men who files reports on everybody else. I can smell them a mile off. We had them during the war.'

Rosie choked back a laugh.

'I see, and why would the Major be spying here?'

Maggie Morgan's friend leaned close. She pursed her lips and screwed up her small black eyes.

'That,' she confided in a loud whisper, 'is for you and me to discover, isn't it, dear?'

3

A deep frown furrowed Andy's brow the next morning as they sat down to breakfast.

'Mum, I have to find some tadpoles for my nature project,' he informed Rosie, 'so I can watch them met . . . meta . . . '

'Metamorphose,' Rosie supplied. 'It means change into another form.'

'Yes, well, I have to do that and then write about it, but first I have to find the tadpoles. Will you take me to the dam today?'

Rosie popped a fried egg on to his plate.

'You know perfectly well that I'll be in the shop all morning,' she reminded him. 'I have to work hard to make a living for us both, Andy.'

'I know, Mum, but it's Saturday. You close the shop at one. Can't we go after lunch?'

Rosie sighed. She had hoped to get that cataloguing done this afternoon.

'I'm sure it can be arranged. Where will you put the tadpoles once we've found them?'

'Tommy said he'll lend me his old fish tank. He'll give me some of his water plants, too. I'll put some rocks in the tank as well, for when they turn into frogs. They can hop on to the rocks so they don't drown. We'll collect the tadpoles in a bottle first, and then put them in the tank, and when the tadpoles have turned into frogs I'll let them go in the garden. Don't worry, Mum, we won't have them jumping all over the flat.'

'Right. We'll take a flask and some sandwiches and have our lunch on a rug next to the water. Why not take your butterfly net along as well? You might see something interesting.'

'Gee, thanks, Mum. I'll clean my room while you're at work.'

Hastily Andy swallowed the last of his toast and dashed off to find a jam jar.

Rosie washed the dishes and left them on the rack to dry. She would have to schedule that cataloguing for another time, one evening when he was in bed, perhaps.

She'd had to work ever since Andy was a few weeks old because there had really been no option. She'd just been widowed and no longer had a husband to support her. Naturally she'd suffered the usual feelings of guilt about it until she'd realised that it was probably healthy for children to see a mother who worked. What wasn't healthy, however, was for them to see a mother who put her work first! And she would never do that. She loved Andy too much.

Rosie went into the bedroom to make her bed. True to her word, Lucy had organised the delivery of two beds the previous day, and what a pleasure it had been to have a good night's sleep!

Business was slow for the first hour but word spread quickly and soon Rosie was kept busy as various members of the community, mostly women, popped in to see what she had on sale. One or two mentioned house sales coming up in the nearby town of Estcourt. Rosie wrote down the details and thanked them delightedly. By the end of the month she would need to replenish some of her stock, and one never knew what one could find at these sales.

It was ten minutes before closing time when two youths sauntered through the door. They stopped just inside and sized her up with stony stares. Both wore grubby overalls, as though they'd just come from their work, and they smelled of sawdust. Trying not to feel ill at ease, Rosie smiled brightly.

'Can I help you?'

The taller one with ginger hair looked at her in an insulting fashion.

'Naa. Wouldn't want to buy any of this junk.'

'Shouldn't think you'll be staying in business for very long,' the other youth added with a sly grin.

He was small and dark, with two scars along one cheek.

'Why don't you just move out?' he suggested nastily. 'We know someone who'd rent this property tomorrow.'

'I have no intention of closing my shop,' Rosie retorted, 'and every intention of making a success of this business. If you are not interested in buying anything, perhaps you'd both be so kind as to leave.'

'We'll leave when we're good and ready,' the tall one sneered, and pretended to examine the silver spoons arranged on a small inlaid table near the door. 'Like I said it's just a lot of junk.'

His companion agreed loudly.

'It's a disgrace, selling rubbish like this to the public.'

Deliberately he hooked a foot through the table leg, overturning both table and contents.

'Come on, Kevin, let's go.'

When they'd gone, Rosie found herself shaking in anger. Despicable louts! She would try to find out who they were and refuse them entry next time. She righted the table and its contents and went to fetch a brush and pan to sweep up the broken Royal Stafford bone china plate which had shattered on the wooden floor. It had been one of her favourites, too.

At one o'clock sharp she locked her doors, counted her takings and took the internal staircase up to the flat. Andy had not only tidied his bedroom, he'd removed all his toys from the living-room and made an effort to wash the kitchen floor.

'It's a bit slushy, Mum,' he greeted her.

Not wishing to discourage his efforts, Rosie surveyed the soapy puddles on the floor and hid a smile.

'You've done a good job,' she applauded, reaching into a cupboard for the mop. 'Why don't you find your butterfly net while I make us a picnic?'

'OK.'

As Andy ran off, Rosie reflected that

she could have done worse for a son. He needed a firm hand as boys usually did, but he was loving and generally very easy-going. She had done her best to provide him with love and security but there were times she longed for someone else to lean on; a solid man with whom she could share the responsibility of bringing up a child. Somehow the secret knowledge that her son was someone else's child and not her own increased that feeling of responsibility.

'Even if I wanted to, I'm not likely to find a father for Andy in a village this size, either,' she told herself briskly as she buttered the bread.

One man's image rose before her, but the thought was so preposterous that she thrust it aside fiercely.

It was very pleasant at the dam. The autumn sun was gentle on their backs as they tucked into tuna sandwiches, boiled eggs, apples and fruitcake. Rosie, wearing a pair of bright pink trousers with her white cotton top, stretched out on the tartan rug and dusted the crumbs off her lap.

'Shall we see about those tadpoles now?' she suggested.

Andy jumped up eagerly, bottle in hand.

'If we don't find any at the edge of the dam, Mum, we'll have to go upstream, near those houses over there. Tommy says there are quiet places in the stream where the frogs spawm.'

'Spawn,' Rosie corrected. 'Right. Lead the way.'

They spent the following half hour messing about in the mud and getting happily damp. Andy collected a dozen tadpoles in the bottle and proudly bore them back to the rug.

'I'll start writing up about 'em tonight,' he informed his mother eagerly. 'Mrs Henderson says she's going to give a prize for the best project. I might win it,' he added ingenuously.

Rosie poured orange juice into two mugs and handed one to her son.

'That would be nice. Collecting the tadpoles was fun, wasn't it? I — '

She broke off in consternation as a noisy yellow missile appeared from nowhere. It barked in delight as it hurled itself upon Andy, smothering him with wet licks. With a startled cry he jumped up, dropping the bottle. The tartan rug quickly became awash with tiny black creatures whose tails thrashed furiously as they wriggled about in the fast-disappearing puddle of water. Andy, seeing his precious collection in jeopardy, let out a despairing wail. Furious, Rosie jumped to her feet.

'Get your stupid dog off us,' she yelled.

Grabbing Andy's butterfly net she swiped at the animal in a futile effort to curb its enthusiasm.

'Shoo!'

Dan ignored her. He was too intent on lapping at the puddle of water.

'He'll eat my tadpoles,' Andy cried.

Major McGregor limped towards them, a look of dismay on his face.

'Dan!' he roared. 'Come here!'

Dan gave an uncertain whine and bounded back to his master, then flopped at Josh's feet with an expression of puzzled disappointment on his doggy face.

'I might have known it was your dog!' Rosie accused bitterly.

Josh turned in the direction of her voice.

'Ms Carlisle? Is that you?'

'It certainly is!'

'I apologise for my dog's behaviour. It sounds as though he has caused you some distress.'

'Too right! He gave us the fright of our lives. It really is time you took him in hand!'

Josh's face tightened.

'I'm sorry. I take it you are not alone?'

'No,' Rosie said coldly. 'Andy and I were just having a peaceful drink in the sun when we were accosted by your animal!'

Andy. There was man on the scene

then. Josh's frown deepened.

'My tadpoles,' Andy wailed.

'We'll collect them up again, Andy,' Rosie told her son firmly. 'Give me the bottle.'

She kneeled down, controlled a shudder and began returning the slimy things to their home.

'Now go and top up the jar with some more water.'

'Thanks, Mum,' Andy mumbled, dashing away a tear from his cheek as he ran to the edge of the dam, returning a few seconds later. 'I wonder what kind of frogs they'll turn into?' he asked.

Josh was listening intently. So Andy was her son! He knew an inexplicable feeling of lightness in his heart. He cleared his throat.

'Where exactly did you find the tadpoles, Andy?'

Andy gazed back uncertainly.

'We got some of them from the still part of the stream near that cottage with the thatched roof,' he explained.

'Ah, and the others?'

'A bit farther up, near the waterfall.'

'Then my guess is that the ones from the waterfall will turn into the Chirping Frog. That's an orange brown one which says, 'Tik-tik-tik'. The others could be Puddle Frogs. They're those fat, warty little things, Of course, had you found any in the reeds at the edge of the dam, they'd most likely be the Golden Spiny Reed Frog. They're very secretive, you know, with a high-pitched call, like this.' He imitated it. 'Prre-heee.'

Andy's mouth fell open.

'Wow,' he whispered with shining eyes.

Andy's mother's mouth had fallen open, too. Was this the same sour, unapproachable man she'd met at the beginning of the week? He was being altogether too amenable, and it made her suspicious. To hide her consternation she bent down and began packing the picnic things.

'We had better be going, Andy,' she said at length. 'I am sure Major

McGregor has better things to do with his time than explain about frogs.'

Andy's face dropped.

'Aw, Mum.'

'I have a suggestion,' Josh intervened smoothly. 'Why not come up to my cottage? It's the one with the thatched roof. Give me an opportunity to make amends for my dog's regrettable behaviour by giving you afternoon tea. I'll tell you about the nightjars outside my window.'

'Cool,' Andy responded. 'What's your dog's name, Major McGregor?'

Josh gave a small grin.

'Dan. He's a little over-enthusiastic at times. You see, he's particularly fond of boys, and he has the heart of a lion.'

Andy turned an awed gaze upon Dan.

'Does he really have a lion's heart?'

'No. It's a figure of speech, Andy,' Rosie explained.

She folded up the tartan rug.

'It's very kind of you, Major, but we won't trouble you for any tea.'

'Please, Mum,' Andy pleaded. 'I'd really like to see where Dan sleeps, and Major McGregor is so interesting. He knows all about frogs and birds and things.'

'We should really be getting home, Andy. I have those meatballs to make, remember?'

'I don't want,' Andy began, and paused.

That would be a lie, and Mum didn't like him to tell lies. He did want meatballs for supper. Trouble was, even more than meatballs, he wanted to go with Major McGregor.

'I have some steak in the freezer,' Josh mentioned in a casual voice. 'You could stay for dinner as well. We could have a barbecue, if you wouldn't mind giving me a little assistance with the salad.'

For some reason Rosie found her heart performing circus tricks inside her chest. She wanted to say yes, but they really ought not to bother a blind man with having to feed them.

Josh sensed her reluctance.

'I'd be delighted to have some company,' he added, managing to sound a little wistful.

Rosie's soft heart yielded. Why hadn't she realised it? The man was lonely!

'Well, if it's no inconvenience?' she asked doubtfully.

'None at all.'

Rosie shot a quick glance at Andy, who was happily engaged in telling Dan what a wonderful dog he was. She decided it would do no harm to make the Major's day, and her son's.

'In that case, we accept. Thank you.'

Josh nodded.

'Andy can help me with the fire.'

Was it her imagination or did those grey eyes gleam with something like satisfaction?

'Let's go, then. Like I said, it's the white cottage with the thatched roof, the one nearest the stream.'

Rosie wondered how he knew the cottage was white. She placed Andy's jar of tadpoles inside the car and locked the picnic things in the boot of the Volkswagen before turning to follow the other two. She looked up, astounded to see that her son had quite naturally slipped his small, grubby hand into Major McGregor's large one and was chatting animatedly as they negotiated the well-worn path together. Rosie hurried to close the gap between them and overheard Andy's next question.

'Can't you see very well, Major McGregor?'

'I'm afraid not, Andy.'

'Why not?'

'I had an accident.'

'What sort of accident?'

Rosie cringed at her son's inquisitiveness. She'd have to teach him that it was impolite to question strangers in that fashion. Despite her embarrassment she found herself listening avidly for the answers.

'I fell out of an aeroplane.'

'Gosh!' Andy whispered and stared up at him in fascinated horror. 'That's cool! Wait till I tell Tommy.'

Josh moved his stick from side to side as he neared the terrace steps.

'Who's Tommy?'

'He's my best friend. Do you have a best friend, Major?'

Josh hesitated.

'Not any more.'

He was not a man to hold grudges. He'd long since come to terms with Geoff Pearson's betrayal. He even found it within himself to wish him well in his new life with Gina, but he no longer counted him as a friend.

Andy began to chatter about frogs, and Rosie gave a sigh of relief. The Major was touchy about his blindness. She would warn Andy to be more tactful in future, if there was a future. She found herself fearing that there would be. It was strange. From the moment she'd laid eyes on Major McGregor she'd been attracted to him. Despite his prickly manner she'd wanted to know more about him. He was a compelling man who both disturbed and intrigued her. At the same time she needed to keep him at arm's length. Much as she would love to have someone to share the responsibility of raising Andy, she dared not permit it. If she re-married, she would have to come clean, and things were complicated enough as it was.

Sensing her presence behind them, Josh turned.

'Ms Carlisle? Welcome to Bergview Cottage. Come inside and make yourself at home.'

He stood politely to one side as they entered.

'Thank you.'

Rosie looked about her with interest. The living-room was large, neat and completely impersonal. The furniture was functional and well-spaced, obviously in order to accommodate an unsighted man, and the walls were bare. She itched to rearrange the furniture and add a few homely touches, a water colour here and a vase of flowers there.

'Sit down while I make the tea,' Josh

invited smoothly.

Rosie sat on the brown leather sofa and beckoned Andy to do the same as Josh discarded his stick and limped into the kitchen to switch on the kettle. Rosie bent her head to hear what Andy was saying and in doing so missed the satisfied grin which flitted across Josh's face.

Never let it be said that Major Joshua McGregor was one to let the grass grow under his feet, he reflected smugly as he set three mugs on a tray. A small voice then queried his motives. Josh replied that his reasons for inviting the lady into the privacy of his home were purely work-related and nothing else. He had no use for a woman otherwise. Women were fickle creatures. He was simply taking advantage of an opportunity which had presented itself.

But the voice persisted. Explain yourself, it mocked. Josh replied that yes, he would. He was expecting a visit from his colonel in a week's time, at which meeting the old man would demand to be given a personal debriefing rather than the more convenient method of a written report not, he added, that the old codger could expect any maps or photographs from a man with partial sight. He would have to be satisfied with an audio tape or two.

Josh then told the voice to shut up, because getting to know this woman here was all part of the job. He had to make reports on people, didn't he? He opened the cupboard above his head. There ought to be some chocolate biscuits in there somewhere. Josh found the packet and opened it.

He and the colonel both knew the whole thing was a farce, anyway. He'd not been deceived when the old man had made his little speech about Josh serving his country in a new capacity, and he wasn't deceived, either, when he'd been informed that the old man was now making a special trip to see him, when all along Josh knew he'd already planned to holiday in the Drakensbergs at this time of the year.

Josh felt for the canister and opened it. He extracted a couple of teabags and popped them into a teapot.

The trouble was, he hadn't much to report. The whole exercise was nothing more than a scheme his superior officer had cooked up in order to give him something to occupy his mind; something which would take him out of his own problems and force him to interact with the community. Until his sight returned he would be unable to resume his career as it had once been. Even then, he would need to undergo a rigorous physical examination before he declared himself completely fit. He had done a good deal of soul-searching in the dark hours of the night and he didn't even know if he wanted to pick up where he'd left off. In the past he'd allowed himself to become too driven. Surely it was time now to smell the roses. He had a further three months in which to consider his options, by which time he would be required to make a serious decision.

Josh had always been a fighting man. To change course now would require a major shift, one which he lacked the motivation to make. Perhaps if he could discover a new direction in life, he'd be moved to take it. But Intelligence! Never in all his born days had he seen himself as a spy.

He gave a resigned sigh and opened the refrigerator for the milk.

Because this was peacetime, he would be required to deliver seemingly innocuous, in-depth reports, not on the political situation but on the various members of the community and its topography, all of which would be fed eventually to the country's National Intelligence Unit. Boring work! He didn't fancy sitting in pubs listening to conversations and asking questions. It simply wasn't his style.

He emptied the packet of biscuits on to a plate and added them to the tray, then carefully picked it up. A small smile played about his mouth as he considered that there were always ways and means to liven up a boring job, like chatting up a lady! To be completely honest she had been on his mind all week. She was the only person in the whole darned place he was interested in finding out about. In fact, he'd like to know her very well indeed, and not least because she had a positively delightful young son.

It was a pity, he reflected ruefully, that he'd been too wrapped up in his career to have settled down and produced a son of his own, always supposing he'd found a woman he could trust, that is.

For the first time ever, Josh began to realise what he'd missed out on.

4

Smoke from the barbecue lingered on the still air as the last rays of the sun drained from the sky. A bright autumn moon began its journey across an indigo velvet sky, and one or two stars began to flicker. At Josh's instruction Andy transferred the meat to the platter Rosie had given him and carried it carefully inside.

Rosie had had a free rein in the kitchen while Josh supervised Andy at the barbecue. She'd baked a few potatoes as the salad was being prepared and in the freezer she'd found a large tub of ice-cream which would do for their dessert.

Determined to make a contribution, Josh set about laying the table as it was too chilly to eat outdoors. He went to the drawer and located the cutlery, poured the orange juice and then set each glass in its place with a grin of satisfaction because he hadn't disgraced himself by spilling any.

'Food's ready. Sit down, Andy,' Rosie called.

Revealing impeccable manners, Josh seated Rosie, helped Andy into his chair and finally took his own place.

'Andy will give thanks for the meal,' Rosie announced firmly.

Andy was too hungry to argue.

'God is great, God is good, thank you, God, for the food,' he gabbled obligingly, his eyes fixed with great pride on the steak.

The Major had allowed him to help with the cooking and the result looked even better than meatballs! Josh hid a smile.

'A boy after my own heart,' he murmured.

His appetite sharpened by the day spent outdoors, Andy wolfed down his steak and potato, but baulked at the greens.

'No ice-cream, Andy, until all that

salad has been eaten,' Rosie declared in her no-nonsense voice.

'But, Mum, I don't like green stuff.'

'Some animals,' Josh intervened smoothly, 'are meat-eaters, like lions, and some, Andy, like giraffes, can only eat greens. You and I are fortunate, old man. We get to eat both. We're designed to do so, you know. That way we can grow up tall, strong and healthy. We humans need a balanced diet, meat and vegetables.'

Andy eyed with interest Josh's muscled forearms and broad chest.

'How tall are you, Major?'

'Oh, a little over six feet.'

'Will I grow as tall as you if I eat a balanced diet?'

'There's a good chance that you will, Andy. Why not give it a try?'

Andy demolished his salad without another word. Rosie's mouth tightened as she felt the familiar little ache of regret. Too bad Andy didn't have a father. A boy needed a father. When he was older he was bound to ask questions, and then she'd have to tell him all about the man who'd fathered him. She'd have to gloss over the fact that according to Andy's biological mother, his father had been a very wicked man, a man who must never discover that he'd fathered a child.

Rosie removed the empty plates and began to serve three large portions of ice-cream while the coffee was percolating. About to carry the dessert to the table, Rosie felt sudden prickles along her spine. Josh had moved and was standing directly behind her, reaching up into a cupboard for the coffee mugs. She was conscious of the heat radiating from his body and felt an absurd urge to turn around and fling herself into his arms. Angry with herself, she slammed the lid on to the box of ice-cream and tossed the scoop into the sink. It was just as well Major McGregor wasn't a mind-reader.

The senses of unsighted people are said to be very finely tuned. As though he knew what Rosie was thinking, Josh, quite forgetting himself, slowly slid his hands up her arms to her shoulders. Rosie quivered. The shock waves vibrated through her whole body but it was a pleasant shock.

'Major, I — '

'The name is Josh, Rosie,' he said softly. 'May I call you Rosie?'

She took a deep breath and examined the cupboard in front of her as though her life depended on it. She was suddenly scared. It was a long time since she'd had this kind of reaction to a man's touch and she wasn't sure if she was ready for it or even desired it.

He knew, she thought, what effect his nearness was having on her, and she could just see the satisfied, little smile playing about his lips. But Josh's eyes held only wary surprise. A bland mask descended as he stepped back, allowing Rosie to regain her composure. She shot him a fierce look, picked up the bowls and dumped them on the table. She had absolutely no intention of making a fool of herself over Major Josh McGregor!

He may have exhibited a flattering interest in her all evening, but that didn't mean a thing, she told herself sternly. What lonely male wouldn't pay considerable attention to the woman he was entertaining? His questions, too, had been subtle, with the unfortunate result that she'd unwittingly revealed more than she should have. He was astute enough to put two and two together concerning certain things she wished to keep private. In future she would be well advised to watch her runaway tongue!

Not only her tongue, she decided, but her mind and emotions as well. As for her body, she'd ignore its signals altogether. She could not afford to get involved with anyone, no matter how much she yearned for it. She had Andy to think of. She had her son to protect. The Major had all but said he was lonely, hadn't he? And lonely, sightless people tended to take more than a passing interest in the people they met. No, it meant nothing, really.

A tangle of emotions rolled through her. It was so long since she'd felt desired that one touch from his hands and she'd felt like butter melting in the sun. It made her uneasy. She liked to be in control. She needed to stay in control, for Andy's sake.

As soon as the coffee mugs were decently cold, Rosie collected them up and made noises about leaving.

'But first I'll wash the dishes.'

'No way,' Josh objected. 'You'll do no such thing.'

'But it'll only take a minute.'

They couldn't very well leave him with a sink full of dirty dishes.

Josh hid his amusement.

'I am perfectly able to wash the dishes, Rosie,' he assured her, guessing her thoughts. 'I'll see you to your car.'

Rosie's face fell.

'Oh, but there's no need,' she objected. 'It's dark and you might lose your way. You might fall and injure yourself.'

Josh was all at once stern and remote.

'I'll not lose my way, and I'll not fall. I have Dan.'

He marched them down the path to the dam and Rosie, conscious of his well-concealed anger, thanked him with nothing more than a relieved, 'Good-bye.'

She drove home along the quiet road with a sleepy Andy in the seat beside her, clutching his precious jar of tadpoles to his chest.

'The Major's cool,' he murmured as he tried to keep his eyes from closing. 'When can we see him again, Mum?'

'I'm not sure, Andy,' Rosie hedged. 'We'd have to wait for an invitation.'

With any luck, no such thing would be forthcoming.

Rosie drove into the main street of the village, turned into her little driveway and parked her car in the garage behind the shop. She inserted the key in the lock, turned on the light and ushered Andy inside.

'Straight to bed, love.'

For once Andy didn't argue. He placed the tadpoles on a kitchen top, brushed his teeth and was asleep almost before his head touched the pillow.

Rosie pottered about in the kitchen, washing the picnic things and setting the table for breakfast before taking herself to her bedroom. She intended to have a nice hot shower and because the next day was Sunday, a long lie in. She collected up her nightdress, entered the bathroom, and stood blinking like an idiot.

'What on earth?'

Rosie stared for a full ten seconds, trying to understand, her mind completely numb. Someone had written a message on the mirror, using her best red lipstick. It was a nasty message, too. It made her skin crawl.

We don't want you in this village. Go away.

Angrily, Rosie reached for a wet face

cloth, intent on scrubbing the mirror clean. She had no idea who had written the words, but if they thought she would be intimidated by such an action, they could think again! She had given a lot of thought to the matter before finally returning to the village of Winterberg and she wasn't about to be scared off that easily.

After her shower she climbed wearily under her duvet. It wasn't a happy feeling to know that someone else had a key to her flat, but she wouldn't allow herself to panic. It was a situation, she reminded herself, which could be easily remedied. There was a locksmith in the village and she would have the locks changed first thing on Monday morning.

* * *

Josh finished his Sunday lunch, tidied the kitchen as best he could and went to find his walking-stick.

'We're going into the village again

this afternoon, Dan,' he told his dog.

Dan pricked up his ears. He gave an obliging bark and ran to have his lead attached to his collar.

'Truth is,' Josh confided as they negotiated the lane a moment later, 'I'd like to see Rosie's shop and get the lie of the land. She said it was in the main street, two doors down from the supermarket. We know where the supermarket is. Rosie's Treasures shouldn't be too difficult to find.'

He and Dan reached the village half an hour later, having encountered no Volkswagens or any other vehicles on the way. It was a warm afternoon and Josh decided that he would stop for a drink on the way back. It was time he revisited the bar at the Mountain View Hotel where hopefully he'd be able to pick up a little more information, and not only for his report. He was determined to discover the identity of a certain two youths.

He'd been amazed at his own furious reaction, well-concealed of course, on hearing how they had entered Rosie's shop and been verbally abusive, not to mention the valuable broken china. The anger had been followed by a familiar feeling of helplessness. If only he had his sight!

Josh recognised the supermarket by the outline of the building and the sounds issuing from it, and went inside. With the assistance of the obliging owner he bought himself a block of cheese and continued along the street, carefully counting the doors.

'Here it is, Dan. Rosie's shop,' he told the dog, standing close to the window and peering inside in the hopes of being able to make out some item on display, but, frustrated at not being able to distinguish much beyond a few dark shapes, he turned away.

There was a crunching sound underfoot. Josh paused.

'Wait, Dan,' he ordered, 'there's a lot of glass around.'

He swept the pavement with his stick and listened to the tinkle of scattering glass. Then he bent down, felt around and picked up a piece.

'Too thick for a bottle. I wonder . . . '

He turned to the window of Rosie's shop and carefully swept a palm over its surface. He soon encountered what he'd guessed must be there.

'Rosie's in a spot of trouble, Dan,' he murmured, 'and I doubt she knows it. Come along.'

He knew she and Andy lived above the shop. He would have to find the staircase around the back. He located the end of the building and guessed it to be the entrance to Rosie's driveway. He and Dan climbed the stairs to the flat above and rang the bell, but after the third ring it was obvious there was no-one at home. Frustrated, Josh leaned against the wall.

'Darned woman's out,' he growled. 'We'll have to wait.'

But at that moment Rosie's car roared into the yard, and Josh grinned.

'That sounds like her.'

Rosie ran up the stairs, feeling in her

pocket for the key to the flat. She'd hurried back after dropping Andy at Tommy's house, reluctant to spend any further time away in case the graffiti artist decided to pay her another visit. Monday morning, and her new lock couldn't come quickly enough! She glanced up, key in hand, and gasped.

'Major McGregor!'

'Josh,' he reminded her. 'Good afternoon, Rosie. I'm not sure what kind of day it is, but it certainly feels warm to me.'

'What do you want?' Rosie asked, quite forgetting her manners.

'I take it you know you have a hole in your window.'

Rosie blinked.

'Window? Which window?' she said, completely taken by surprise.

'Downstairs.'

'The shop? Oh, good grief.'

She inserted the key into the lock.

'You'd better come in while I take a look.'

Josh followed her inside, careful to

use his stick in case he encountered an obstacle in the hallway. Rosie tossed him a rueful glance.

'There's nothing you can fall over. I've hardly had time to accumulate any furniture. Have a seat. It's through there, in the living-room.'

She turned and disappeared down the internal staircase to the shop.

There was indeed, a big, gaping hole, and glass everywhere.

'Calm down, Rosie,' she ordered, taking a deep breath. 'There's no need to get twitchy. Be brave, stand your ground. Nobody's going to be allowed to turn you out of here.'

Lying on the floor, mercifully having missed the display of china in a glass-fronted cabinet nearby, lay the brick which had been hurled through the window. Rosie eyed it miserably. It was beyond a joke! Her first week in the village and she'd already been invaded twice, not to mention these two objectionable lads.

'I suppose I ought to inform the

police in Estcourt,' she sighed, and picked up the telephone.

'Name?' the duty officer enquired tersely.

'Rosemary Carlisle.'

'Address?'

'Rosie's Treasures, Main Street, Winterberg.'

Quickly she explained her predicament.

'Don't touch anything, miss. We'll be right along.'

Feeling dejected, Rosie mounted the stairs, to find Josh standing exactly where she'd left him.

'Well?' he asked.

She tried to make light of her trouble.

'A brick. Fortunately there's not much damage. It's just the window.'

'You're insured?'

'No. I'll have to extend my overdraft in order to have it repaired, and then there's the lock as well.'

'Lock?'

'My door. Someone entered the flat

yesterday while we were at the dam. I'll need to change the lock.'

Josh's jaw hardened.

'And?'

'Nothing was taken. They left a message scribbled in lipstick on my mirror, that's all.'

'Tell me what it said.'

Rosie hesitated. She didn't like burdening other people with her problems. It's what came of having had to take care of herself for so long.

'Oh, something to the effect that I wasn't wanted in this village.'

'I'll get to the bottom of this,' he promised.

Rosie gave a reluctant smile. It was sweet of the man, but what possible help could he be?

'That's good of you, but I'll manage. Would you like a cup of coffee?'

Josh reached for his stick.

'No, thank you. Dan and I have other business in the village.'

He stood up, tossed an unfocused glance in her direction and told her quietly, 'You will have to point me in the direction of the door.'

Rosie curled her fingers around his arm.

'This way.'

Immediately, Josh covered her fingers with one hand. He had a sudden, inexplicable urge to take her into his arms and protect her from the whole world, and it shook him to the core. This is what came of no longer having a woman to care for, he supposed. He was the type of man who needed to cherish a woman, but he must remember that Rosie was not his woman.

'Right, Dan,' Josh informed his dog when they reached the street, 'we have work to do. I may only be half the man I used to be, but where there's a will, there's a way. I hope you can hold your drink, because we are about to spend the next few hours listening to inane chatter in a public house.'

He grinned to himself as he prodded the pavement with his stick.

'With any luck we'll be able to pick

up a lead or two. I am keen to find out who is harassing Rosie.' He added, 'It's a happy fact that when people see a blind man they automatically imagine him to be deaf as well.'

★ ★ ★

Andy and Tommy were at that moment perched in the oak tree in Tommy's garden, happily engaged in nailing a piece of board to a branch.

'I bet this tree house'll be better'n Davey's and Craig's,' Tommy stated.

'Yeah. Ours is higher than theirs,' Andy pointed out in satisfaction.

'Ours is too high for wild animals, so we're all right but they'll have to watch it. The lions'll get their food.'

'Cool,' Andy sighed.

'They needn't think we'll let 'em have any of our cookies if they're hungry,' Tommy added.

'No way! My mum bakes the best cookies in Winterberg.'

'My mum says your mum needs a

man. You haven't got a Dad, have you?' Tommy said thoughtfully.

Andy looked up quickly.

' 'Course I've got a Dad,' he retorted.

'Haven't,' Tommy said, determined to prove he was right.

'Have!'

'Where is he, then?'

Andy considered for a moment.

'He lives by the dam, an' he's got a dog called Dan, a great big yellow one. An' my dad fell out of an aeroplane!'

Tommy looked sceptical.

'Didn't.'

'Did! He's even got a sore leg to prove it.'

'Show me your dad, then,' Tommy taunted. 'Show me his sore leg.'

'I will.'

'When?'

Andy threw down the hammer. It missed the board and bounced all the way down through the leaves to the grass. 'Now,' he yelled.

Tommy was taken aback.

'Now?'

'Yes. I'll take you there right now, to the dam, an' I'll show you my dad. Let's go.'

Tommy eyed him nervously.

'Like, right now? How'll we get there?'

'Walk,' Andy retorted, crossing his fingers behind his back. 'I know the way. I went to my dad's house last night and we had steak. You're not a scaredy cat, are you?'

Tommy hated to lose face.

'All right,' he agreed unhappily, 'we'll go, but we'd better not tell my mum. She'll say no.'

The boys scrambled down from the tree, sneaked past the house and let themselves quietly out of the front gate.

5

Josh found his way to the Mountain View Hotel and entered the bar with Dan at his heel.

'Good afternoon, Major,' Daniel Allbright greeted him, unobtrusively guiding him to an empty table. 'Nice to see you again. What can I get you?'

Josh placed his order and asked after Daniel's wife. Now that he knew the Allbrights were related to Rosie, he found himself taking an interest in their lives. Daniel hid his surprise.

'Lucy? She's coping. Gets a little tired these days, but that's understandable. I keep telling her to rest up a bit more, but she's rather stubborn. It's our first, you know. It'll be great to be a father.'

Josh agreed politely but the smile did not quite reach his eyes. If the truth be told, he was rather envious of the man, and it was a new sensation. Ever since he had met Rosie Carlisle there had been an unaccustomed twisting in his stomach, a wholly unfamiliar and inexplicable attraction towards domesticity. He now faced a compelling urge to care for someone other than himself, a woman he could treat like a queen. He had never experienced the like before, and it was very disturbing.

It was no use pretending any longer. His priorities had changed vastly in the last few months and he wasn't ashamed to admit it. He wanted a wife. He wanted a son. The trouble was, he'd left things too late. In his present state he had nothing left to offer a woman.

He couldn't understand it. He'd been so involved in his career that he'd never really given much thought to remarriage, let alone producing a family, but now that they were nothing but a pipe dream, he wanted them desperately. Fatherhood — the word had a good, solid ring to it. If ever he had a son, he wanted one like young Andy Carlisle.

His next thought, understandably, was of Andy's mother. Ever since she'd all but demolished him on the road to the village he hadn't been able to get her out of his mind. For the first time in many months Josh felt as though he was beginning to care about life again.

★ ★ ★

Andy and Tommy made their way through the village and continued along the road which wound its way in the direction of the mountains.

'How much farther is it, Andy?' Tommy asked apprehensively after they had been walking for some minutes.

He hadn't bargained on having to travel quite so far to see Andy's Dad! Andy indicated vaguely, for distances meant nothing to him.

'It's along this road. There's a stream near the house, with frogs in it. That's where I got my tadpoles.'

Tommy brightened.

'If we can find a bottle or a tin, I'd like some, too.'

'OK, but we have to walk fast so we can get there before dark,' Andy reminded him.

'Dark? I don't like it when it's dark.'

'Don't worry, Tommy. We'll climb up a tree so the lions won't get us.'

They walked in silence for another twenty minutes. Finally Andy stopped.

'I can hear a stream,' he said. 'It's over there, through that bit of bush. Let's go and have a drink, Tommy. I'm thirsty.'

'We might even find some tadpoles,' Tommy said.

He followed Andy, plunging into the waist-high foliage. Together they fought their way through a thicket towards the sound of water.

'There it is,' Andy panted triumphantly as he peered through a forest of reeds and grasses at the silver cascade.

They waded into the shallows, cupped their hands and took their fill of the clear, cool water. Walking had been thirsty work! The temptation to linger was strong. The boys took off their shoes, tied the laces together and spent the next hour wading up and down the stream. They found sticks with which to stir up the mud and competed happily in races with floating leaves which they followed downstream, cheering. Eventually Tommy noticed the sky.

'It's getting dark, Andy. Look, the sun's setting! I'm cold, too.'

'Huh?'

'It's getting dark and I'm cold,' Tommy repeated.

Andy looked about him in dismay.

'Jeepers. We'd better be going then, Tommy.'

But which way? The thicket didn't look quite the same any more. They must have come a long way downstream without realising it. Hastily scrambling from the water and tying on their shoes, the boys paused to survey the landscape in complete bewilderment.

'The road's this way,' Andy guessed,

sounding more confident than he felt. 'Hurry, Tommy.'

After a further ten minutes' bashing through the bush Andy's confidence evaporated. He was compelled to acknowledge defeat. He and Tommy were tired, wet and hungry and the road was nowhere in sight. Andy swallowed hard to keep the lump from his throat.

'Tommy,' he said carefully, 'I think we're lost.'

Tommy gave a despairing wail.

'I knew it! We'll be eaten by lions and they'll crunch our bones an' nobody'll ever find us.'

He began to sob. Andy patted him awkwardly on the back.

'Don't worry, Tommy. We'll spend the night in a tree, just like I said.'

He looked around hopefully and spotted a sturdy-looking mahogany tree.

'This one'll do.'

He gave Tommy another encouraging pat and began to climb.

★ ★ ★

Josh finished his drink and drummed his fingers on the table. He was fully prepared to sit there the whole evening if need be, listening intently to the conversations going on around him. He had an excellent memory, so storing up items of information was no problem. He needed as much information as possible for his debriefing in a few days' time when the colonel would expect a decent intelligence report, and Josh fully intended to play out the charade to the hilt, if for no other reason than to keep the boredom at bay.

He considered some of the seemingly innocuous stuff he would be required to deliver and felt nothing but distaste. He wasn't really interested in which individuals favoured which side of the political spectrum and couldn't care less about their daily routines or the state of their finances. Then there was the topography. He was required to deliver information concerning the terrain, where the village water supply was situated, where the electricity installations were housed.

Were there well-worn paths across the borders with other countries? Were there any broken fences which would indicate easy or illegal access? He gave a wry smile. With his present disability he couldn't very well sit somewhere at night in camouflage clothing with a pair of infra-red binoculars, could he? Much less keep a watch on the movements of the locals! But he could use his ears, like now.

Ordering Dan to stay, Josh moved to the bar where he asked for another soft drink. He preferred not to use alcohol when he needed his wits about him. As he reached for the glass, he was deliberately jostled on the elbow. The sticky liquid sloshed over his clothing, swirled across the counter and spilled on to his fine leather shoes.

'Sorry,' the ginger-haired youth on his right sniggered.

'Too bad he can't see what he's

doing, eh, Kevin?' his friend smirked.

Josh lifted his glass, drank what was left and set it back on the counter.

'You must be Kevin Petty,' he said casually, turning to the youth. 'Your father is Sam Petty, the joiner.'

'How did you know that?' the youth asked in astonishment.

'Oh, I keep my eyes open,' Josh informed him blandly.

Kevin Petty regarded him in puzzlement.

'But I thought you were blind.'

Josh hid a grin. Not too bright, our Kevin.

'Besides,' he continued, 'you smell of sawdust.'

Daniel Allbright approached the counter, took in the situation and swiftly mopped up the mess. He darted Josh a look of compassion.

'Another drink, Major? On the house this time.'

He replaced Josh's glass and hurried away to serve another customer. Kevin's eyes narrowed.

'Who are you, anyway? He called you Major. Major who?'

'McGregor,' Josh clipped. 'And your friend is?'

'Paul,' Kevin supplied reluctantly. 'Paul White. Works for my dad.'

'I hear,' Josh said casually, 'that your father is looking for more premises in order to expand the business. Is that true?'

'What's it to you?' Paul White chipped in rudely.

Josh ignored him.

'I'm told that business is booming. You'll be needing a bigger timber yard, I imagine.'

'Yeah,' Kevin said smugly. 'Business is great. We're the best in town.'

'Why doesn't your father rent or buy one of the properties adjacent to his existing premises if he wishes to expand?'

Josh made the suggestion in a reasonable voice, as though the thought had only just occurred to him. Kevin's expression turned belligerent.

'That's exactly what we planned to do, only this stupid female went and moved in under our noses, see.'

'Oh? Which female?'

A few pints of beer had loosened Kevin's tongue.

'The tart with the fancy junk she calls antiques. Rosie someone or other. She says she's not moving, but me and Paul have ways and means.'

'What ways and means?' Josh asked in a manner which said he wasn't really interested.

Paul slammed down his empty glass.

'It's none of your business! Come on, Kev, let's go. You talk too much.'

He grabbed his friend by the elbow and marched him away. Josh put down his drink. It was exactly as he'd thought. These were the yobs who were harassing Rosie. His jaw clenched in frustration. He would have to be content with biding his time. It was a pity he did not have the full use of his eyes and limbs, for it would give him great pleasure to teach them a lesson they were unlikely to forget. He found his stick and groped for Dan's lead.

'Come on, old son, we need to be on our way.'

Outside on the pavement, he enquired the time from a passerby, dismayed to find that the sun had already set. As a rule he avoided having to walk home in the dark, mindful of his impaired visibility. He donned his red baseball cap, tightened his grip on Dan's lead and set out. On reaching the top of the hill he was forced to stop and rest. Six months ago he would have been able to run a marathon with no problem at all. Now he was having to catch his breath after ten minutes.

He pressed on, remaining alert for any vehicles. He might not be able to say what make they were but at least he could distinguish their lights in the darkness. After a further ten minutes, the ache in his hip forced him to take another rest.

'Hold it, Dan,' he gasped.

But Dan, for once in his life, was disposed to disobey the master. He was busy sniffing the air, ears upright, every sense alert.

'What is it, Dan?'

Dan gave a sudden, joyous bark and took off into the undergrowth. Josh, lurching after him, was caught unawares by the sudden movement, carried along by the momentum.

'Dan!' he yelled, dropping his stick, but Dan had other fish to fry.

He continued, dragging Josh with him. Josh stumbled blindly over an anthill protruding from the vine-tangled scrub, lost his balance and pitched headlong into a pile of boulders. Blood trickled down his temple as a blanket of utter darkness engulfed him.

★   ★   ★

Jean Mitchell, Tommy's mother, went to call the boys inside. They'd spent the whole afternoon playing happily in the tree house and now it was almost time for Rosie Carlisle to fetch her son.

'Tommy,' she yelled, 'it's time to come inside.'

Puzzled at the silence which ensued, she approached the oak tree and peered up into its branches. She frowned. Where were those tiresome boys? She had just removed a chicken from the oven and needed to make the gravy. With an exclamation of annoyance Mrs Mitchell proceeded to search the rest of her large garden.

'John,' she told her husband worriedly a few moments later, 'I can't find the boys.'

Mr Mitchell kept his eyes on the rugby match he was viewing on the television.

'Look in the shed. They sometimes play in there.'

'I've looked everywhere! John, they've disappeared.'

With a resigned sigh, he got up and switched off the television.

'Don't panic, Jean. They're bound to be somewhere.'

Two minutes later, Rosie arrived to fetch her son. She'd managed to finish the cataloguing in her shop and had even had time to pop a casserole into the oven. Jean Mitchell opened the door and explained tearfully.

'Tommy and Andy have disappeared. John has taken the car and is driving around the village to see if he can spot them.'

'I'll do the same,' Rosie said. 'Have you been over to the neighbours?'

'Yes. No-one's seen hide or hair of them.'

Rosie ran back to the car. Andy, a sensible child, would never go off anywhere without permission, and she'd taught him never to accept lifts or get into a stranger's car. The boys had to be around the village somewhere.

★ ★ ★

Tommy gave a quiet sob as he clung to a stout branch.

'I'm cold and I'm hungry, Andy.'

'Me, too,' Andy replied in a small voice.

It was all his fault. He should have known they'd get lost, but he'd really, really wanted to show Tommy his dad. Well, not his real dad, exactly, but his pretend dad. He wasn't going to tell Tommy that, of course. He wasn't about to admit that he didn't know his real dad because Tommy might feel sorry for him.

A sudden sound jerked him upright. It was a crashing sort of sound, like an animal running through the long grass. Andy froze in terror.

'What's that noise?' Tommy quavered. 'It's not a lion, is it?'

Andy held his breath. He peered out into the darkness, quite certain that whatever it was, it was heading straight for them. Suddenly the crashing stopped and became a series of short, sharp barks which changed into a whining noise, right beneath their tree.

'Dan!' Andy yelled.

He scrambled down from his branch

and joyously jumped the last few feet
to the ground. He hurled himself at
the Labrador, flinging two small,
sun-browned arms around the dog's
neck.

'Oh, Dan!'

Gingerly Tommy climbed to the
ground.

'Who's Dan?' he asked, having
regained a semblance of bravado.

'Dan's my dad's dog. Isn't he clever?
He's come to find us!'

'Where's your dad, then?'

Andy looked nonplussed for a
moment.

'He must be at home. Dan will take
us there now, won't you, Dan?'

He reached for Dan's lead only to
find it had been mangled by the dog's
headlong flight through the bush.

'You've broken your lead, Dan,' he
scolded, 'but never mind. We'll follow
you. Home, boy!' he ordered in his best
imitation of Josh's voice.

Dan gave a yelp of pure delight. He
understood the word, home, and his

favourite boy was pleased with him. Without a moment's hesitation he plunged in the direction of the cottage.

6

Rosie turned a dark, anxious gaze on Jean Mitchell's face, and said, 'There's just one more place they could have taken themselves off to but I really can't believe they'd do it.'

'Where's that?'

'The dam.'

The other woman gave a low moan.

'Tommy has been telling me all about those tadpoles Andy found there. I suppose they've gone to fetch some more. As soon as John's back, I'll tell him to go out there. I'd better stay here in the house in case they return.'

'No need. I'll go,' Rosie said, snatching up her car keys, giving a shaky smile. 'Don't worry, Jean, they'll turn up. I know they will.'

Josh would be there, Rosie thought in some relief as she ran back to the car. He'd take good care of the boys, and if they weren't there, he'd know what to do.

Once clear of the village Rosie put her foot down on the accelerator, ignoring the speed limit. Once she'd located her son, she told herself fiercely, she'd tear the hide off him! But when she arrived at Josh's cottage and saw two frightened, tearful small boys huddled damply on the doorstep she did nothing of the sort. Instead, she burst into tears.

'I'm sorry, Mum,' Andy apologised in a small voice. 'I won't do it again.'

'I should hope not,' Rosie sniffed, trying to sound severe. 'Why did you boys not tell Mrs Mitchell where you were going?'

Andy and Tommy exchanged looks. Best not to say too much.

'I wanted to show Tommy something,' Andy muttered. 'We were coming here to the cottage and then we got lost, but Dan came and found us.'

'I see. Well, I'd better tell everyone you two are safe and sound.'

She whipped out her mobile phone and quickly relayed the news to Tommy's relieved mother.

'We'll be home shortly,' she added.

The cottage was in darkness. Major McGregor had obviously retired early. It would be just as well not to bother the man, Rosie thought. He was still recuperating, and probably needed all the sleep he could get. Warning them to be quiet, she shepherded the boys to the car, leaving a disappointed Dan curled up on the doorstep.

An hour later, her son, having made his peace with the adults, eaten an enormous quantity of chicken casserole and spent an enjoyable ten minutes in the bath pretending to be a pirate king, fell into an exhausted sleep. Rosie tiptoed into his room, offered a prayer of thanks for his safe return and went to her own bed. Her last thought as she fell asleep was that bringing up a child was not as easy as she'd first supposed. Her thoughts drifted.

From the moment Rosie had first

seen the tiny, dark-haired little baby, she'd wanted him very badly, and blithely unaware of the responsibility entailed, had come to a somewhat unorthodox arrangement with his mother. Rosie had just lost her husband and had needed something to fill the huge, emotional void in her life. From that moment, Andy had become her son. She loved him fiercely and no-one would ever be permitted to take him away, which is doubtless why she spent a restless night dreaming that adoption agency officials were hammering at her door.

When Rosie finally awoke she wondered why her eyeballs had fogged over like a windshield. She blinked, trying to clear the haze. Was it really morning already? She glanced at the luminous face of her bedside clock which reported that it was only six fifteen.

She yawned. It was no good going back to sleep now, so she might as well get up and start her chores. She had a busy day ahead, organising a glazier to fix the window and a locksmith to change the lock. The police had arrived the previous afternoon and advised her to contact the joiner, Sam Petty, to ask him to board up the window until the morning, but what with Andy's disappearance, such things had gone straight out of her head. After all, what was a window compared with her son's safety?

Andy was his usual cheerful self at breakfast, requesting a second helping of bacon and eggs. He gobbled his toast, seemingly keen to get to school, doubtless in order to boast about how clever, brave and resourceful Josh's wonderful dog was. He'd gone on and on about the Labrador during dinner the previous evening, hinting broadly that he would like to go and live with Josh so that he could play with Dan every day.

Rosie sighed. Her son was becoming fixated on Major McGregor and his dog. Oh, she was very grateful to Dan for finding the boys, but that didn't mean she could allow Andy to make a nuisance of himself by paying little visits whenever he pleased. She would have to make it quite clear that Dan and the Major were not to be a regular part of their lives. If need be she would have to buy Andy a dog of his own in order to distract him.

Rosie washed the breakfast dishes while Andy went to clean his teeth.

Andy, she thought ruefully, was not the only one to be thinking constantly about Major McGregor. In fact, he had begun intruding into her own thoughts on a daily basis and she didn't like it one bit. Idly she wondered what he was doing at that very moment.

In fact, Josh McGregor was lying on a very uncomfortable pile of stones, reliving the trauma of his flying accident. He experienced the horror of falling through the air at seventy miles an hour, knowing that he was about to hit the ground. He could even taste the red dust in the back of his throat as he watched the desert rushing up to meet him, and knew with calm certainty that he was going to die.

An enormous thump on the chest caused the breath to gush from his lungs. Something unpleasantly wet plastered itself all over his face and hair. All he could manage was a feeble groan. At the sound, Dan gave a small whine and nudged at his arm with a damp, quivering nose.

'Dan? Is that you?'

Josh struggled to focus. What the dickens was his dog doing here in the Kalahari Desert? And why was he feeling so stiff and cold if he wasn't already dead? He opened his eyes and blinked. He wasn't in the desert at all. He was somewhere in the heart of the Drakensberg because there were mountains in the distance, normally dark and sombre but now washed pink in the early-morning light.

His eyes widened more. It wasn't just any bush surrounding him, it was river bush, thick with reeds, which meant there was water nearby. In fact, he could hear the sound of it. What's more, he could see the dawn filtering through the trees. He could actually see it!

'Well, I'll be second cousin to a monkey,' he said slowly, and grinned.

His eyes feasted for a moment on things he hadn't seen for months. He could even see the veins in the leaves above his head. Josh sat up gingerly. His body ached all over and his head pounded. Remembering his headlong flight after Dan, he reached up and felt the patch of dried blood at his temple. He must have knocked himself out when he'd tripped, thanks to the dog's impulsive behaviour, and the shock of the fall had had exceedingly good results!

'Well, it seems I am still in one piece,' he remarked once he'd managed to stand up.

He had long since stopped wearing a watch because he couldn't make out the figures, but it gave him enormous pleasure now to examine the most minute details of nature around him. The position of the sun told him it must be around six o'clock, which meant that he'd been out cold for hours.

'Come on, Dan,' he ordered. 'You've lost half your lead, I see, but never mind, old chap, this time I can manage without it.'

He gave a sudden, light-hearted chuckle.

'I'm a new man, Dan, except, of course, for the leg, but who cares about that? That fall you caused must have unravelled the wires somewhere. I'm eternally grateful to you.'

Dan gave a happy bark, conscious that something momentous had happened. He bounded about Josh's legs, prancing in excited circles while Josh began to pick his way through the vines and creepers.

'Dan,' Josh said, 'I'd like this to be kept a secret between the two of us, at least for a little while longer. I may have regained my sight but I would prefer it that no-one else knew. There are things I must see to first.'

He whistled all the way home, took a shower and cooked an enormous breakfast of steak and eggs, without mishap, before taking his coffee into the living-room where he sat down calmly to consider his future. His first move would be to determine what Rosie Carlisle actually looked like.

* * *

The glazier waited patiently while Rosie wrote out a cheque and handed it over. It was the second one she'd written this morning, for the locksmith had just called, as well. Both were expenses she had not bargained for.

'There you are, Mr Todd. Thank you for the new window.'

When he had departed she swept up the bits of putty he'd left lying on the floor and took out her spray bottle in order to polish the new window. Satisfied that it looked pristine, she withdrew to the till to count her takings. This was something she did frequently during the day and it gave her great pleasure. It was encouraging to know that she'd made a record number of sales this morning, and she wrapped the knowledge about her like a security blanket. It went some small way to easing the irritation of having had to pay for those repairs.

The bell on the shop door pinged and Josh entered with Dan.

Rosie glanced up and felt the blood rush to her face. She reached up and put her hands against her cheeks. It was as well Major McGregor couldn't view her confusion, she thought, for she was behaving like a silly schoolgirl!

Josh was swinging his stick from side to side in an obvious manner as he negotiated the space between the door and the counter. Rosie felt a wave of tenderness as she watched him, a strong, independent man, coping so well with his disability. The tenderness was followed by a deep yearning to comfort and support him, and it was this yearning which alerted her to the true state of her emotions.

Oh, help, she thought, feasting her eyes on him, this is serious! What was happening to her? An unexpected visit from a man she hardly knew and still wasn't sure she actually liked, and she turned into some alien creature without a logical thought in her head. It was difficult to maintain her composure when every thud of her heart reminded her how attractive she found him. Yes, it was just as well he couldn't observe her reactions.

'Good morning, Rosie,' Josh said in a calm voice which gave away nothing of the sudden jerking of his pulses.

He hadn't missed a thing, and the look on her face had been something to die for. He found himself quite disarmed, especially as she was now trying to appear so nonchalant. He stared at her long and hard, surprise on his face. He hadn't realised that she was quite so exquisite! Remembering that he was supposed to be unsighted, he looked away quickly.

'You said you sell antiques in here. Would you describe them to me?' he begged.

The poor man must be bored today, Rosie thought, which is no doubt why he'd decided to pay her a visit. He was in need of some entertainment. She decided that she'd be happy to oblige, for there were no other customers in the shop at that moment.

'I'd be delighted to.'

Ever happy to share her love of Victoriana, Rosie plunged into descriptions and prices and dates, adding that she hoped to find some worthwhile pieces at a house sale in Estcourt the following week.

Josh watched her through half-veiled grey eyes, enjoying every minute. That hair was wonderful — dark, untamed, just as he'd imagined it would be. What's more, it framed a sweet, classically beautiful face with high cheekbones and a firm, pointed chin.

He watched her lustrous dark eyes light with enthusiasm as she described her treasures, and the sweep of dark lashes fluttering against her cheeks as she cast her eyes from one item to another. Her small, neat hands fluttered about as she spoke, and her voice, low and well modulated, was as seductive as wine. He wondered why such a beautiful woman had not remarried.

Careful to maintain the appearance of disablement, Josh heaved a wistful sigh.

'I wish I could examine some of these items more closely. You make them sound delightful. I must not detain you further, Rosie.'

He watched as her face fell.

'Oh, but you're not detaining me at all. It's not as though I had a shop full of customers right now. It's one o'clock, and I close for an hour. Would you like to come upstairs? I'll make us a sandwich.'

'Thank you, I should like that,' he agreed.

He watched her lock the shop door, hiding a smile. It was sheer joy to follow her graceful movements. She had the body of a dancer. A moment later he accompanied her up the narrow staircase to the flat, followed obediently by a faithful Dan. Just as she'd told him, Rosie's home was sparsely furnished. She seated him in her only armchair in the living-room and advised him to relax while she went to make the lunch. In the kitchen, she switched on the electric kettle and hurriedly assembled a plate of sandwiches. Fetching her small bedside table to place beside him, she then went to fetch one of the kitchen chairs to sit on.

'Your coffee.'

She placed it on the table and lifted his hand in order to guide it towards the mug. Josh's face remained impassive, his reaction to her touch well hidden. He could not, however, suppress the sudden gleam in his eyes. Rosie glanced at his face with a puzzled look in her dark eyes.

'There is something different about you today,' she observed.

Josh shot her a quick glance, deliberately making it appear unfocused.

'Oh? In what way?'

'I'm not sure.' She frowned. 'You seem happier, for a start. You were a sour, bad-tempered individual when I met you, and I thought you were a complete and utter bore. You had all the charisma of a . . . '

She trailed off, conscious that her tongue was about to hurtle out of control again.

'I'm sorry, I didn't mean to be rude.'

Josh stifled a laugh.

'At least you're honest. May I ask you a personal question?'

'Well, yes.'

'Who is Andy's father?'

Rosie gasped.

'What do you mean?'

'You said you'd been a widow for eight years. Andy is not yet seven.'

'My personal life is none of your

business!' she snapped, flushing.

He shrugged.

'You're right. I was out of line. Sorry.'

He looked so meek that Rosie felt quite sorry for him. She relented with a little sigh, quite failing to note the glint of mockery in his eyes.

'Andy's origins are not quite what they seem, but it is not something which I care to discuss. And now, the subject is closed.'

'Yes, ma'am.'

'I'll see you down the back stairs,' she offered.

Josh knew when he was being given his marching orders. He rose, thanked her nicely for the lunch and called Dan to heel, not forgetting to wave his stick about as he followed Rosie to the door. She accompanied him to the bottom of the stairs where she cast a quick look around her small garden.

'Oh, no!'

Her tones alerted Josh to her distress. He followed the direction of her glance and saw for himself. Her little car was standing in the driveway and by the look of it the air in all four tyres had been expelled quite deliberately.

'Something wrong?' he asked, pretending not to see.

'My car!'

Rosie ran to inspect the damage only to discover that not only had the air escaped but the tyres had been slashed and were ruined beyond repair.

'Oh, no,' she reiterated.

At this rate she would face financial ruin within a month! In a voice thick with tears she turned to Josh.

'Someone had slashed my tyres!'

At the sight of her misery Josh quite forgot himself.

'So I see.'

Grimly he surveyed the damage. Then without thinking, he bent to inspect the tyres more closely.

'This one's not too bad, but the others have had it, I'm afraid.'

At the sudden silence, he turned round to find Rosie staring as though he had two heads. Too late he realised what he'd done. Rosie rounded on him, her voice low and furious.

'You're not blind at all, are you? You're nothing but a fraud, a despicable liar! You've been playing on everyone's sympathy. How can you live with yourself?'

Josh opened his mouth and closed it again. Anything he said now would only make matters worse.

'Etta de Wit was right,' Rosie stormed. 'She said it was all a cover! I didn't believe her, but now I can see she was right. You know something? You're nothing but lowlife, Major McGregor! Admit it, you're a spy!'

Josh hid his shock. He had no idea how his cover in the village had been blown. So much, he thought wryly, for his intelligence-gathering abilities! He eyed her warily.

'Yes, I am involved in intelligence work for my country, Rosie, but like your Andy, I'm not what I seem. And believe it or not, I was blind. I have only just regained my sight.'

'How convenient,' Rosie taunted.

'It's true.'

'Then why do I not believe you?'

He shrugged.

'You said there was something different about me today, and you were right. The difference is that I can see again. Last night's fall did it. I knocked myself out on a pile of rocks.'

Rosie gave a cynical laugh.

'And would you care to enlighten me further about this so timely fall?'

'Certainly.'

He lifted a strand of hair at his temple and revealed a recently-dressed graze. Briefly he supplied the details.

'There's one thing I don't understand, though, and that is why Dan left me lying in the bush in order to return to the cottage. It was completely out of character.'

'Returned to the cottage?'

'Yes. Furthermore, he had company. I saw for myself the footprints on my doorstep, three sets of them.'

His steely gaze narrowed on her face.

'If I'm not mistaken, some of them belonged to the Carlisle family, you and your son, Andy. I'm not partial to snoopers, Rosie. I should like an explanation.'

Rosie took a deep breath. He must be telling the truth. The reason the cottage had been in darkness was that he'd been lying unconscious in the bush. And all the time she'd assumed he'd gone to bed early!

'They were Andy's footprints,' she admitted. 'He and Tommy were indeed on your doorstep last night.'

It was her turn to make the explanations.

'They got lost near the stream and Dan found them and took them home to your cottage. I located them there some while after dark. You weren't there, for obvious reasons. I thought you were asleep.'

'Ah. That explains why my dog took off on the road home. He'd caught their scent. It seems I'm indebted to the boys, for without them I would still be sightless.'

Rosie studied him thoughtfully with her dark, velvet eyes. Josh, wishing he could see into her pretty little head, waited with well-hidden impatience. Suddenly Rosie smiled.

'Let's go back inside and decide what to do about this harassment I'm getting, Major,' she suggested. 'If I promise to make you another cup of coffee, will you promise to tell me who you really are?'

An invitation Josh couldn't resist! He held out a large hand.

'Done,' he told her crisply.

She was halfway across the lawn when his next words stopped her.

'On one condition.'

Rosie turned around and eyed him warily.

'And that is?'

'I get to ask some questions of my own.'

Yeah, right, Rosie thought, determined not to divulge a thing.

7

Determinedly, Rosie set the mug of coffee next to Josh's elbow, and immediately said, 'Right, now you'll answer my questions, McGregor. First question — who exactly are you?'

'You already know that,' Josh replied. 'Major Joshua McGregor, South African Air Force. I served at the base in Pretoria until three months ago.'

'Were you dishonourably discharged?'

'Certainly not! Technically I'm on sick leave.'

'I see. What are you really doing in Winterberg? You're surely not here to observe the activities of these innocent people for the fun of it, are you?'

Josh hid a grin.

'You've got it in one, lady. I'm definitely not here for the fun of it! I'm here to recuperate from an accident, and have no more interest in why old

Mrs Dawson has finally decided to have her bunions done than you have, or why the postmistress can't get along with the doctor's wife or why the African staff at the abattoir are ready to strike.'

'Then why do you feel the need to spy on people?'

'Basically, in order to keep an old man happy. My colonel cooked up this idea after my accident, when I was at a very low ebb, for therapeutic reasons, I guess. He decided I needed something to live for, that I needed to feel I was still serving my country. The whole thing was his idea and quite frankly, I thought it stank.'

'What idea?'

'Well, that I become involved in some peace-time intelligence work. Boring stuff, really, not my scene at all. My heart, as they say, is not in it.'

Rosie observed him curiously.

'Then where is your heart?'

Josh hesitated. He couldn't very well expect Rosie to open up about herself if he didn't deliver the goods first, could he? A bargain had been struck, after all.

'I used to be extremely career-minded, Rosie. There was no room for anything else in my life, not even a woman. I'm afraid I drove my wife into the arms of another man. Ditto, my girlfriend.'

'And now?'

'I have no definite plans for the moment. All I can say is that for me, life in the Forces has palled. When one undergoes a near-death experience, one is inclined to re-evaluate one's whole life. I'm seeking a new direction. I would like to continue serving my country, but in a different capacity.'

He put down his mug.

'Now let's talk about you, Rosie. What do you want out of life?'

Rosie gulped down her coffee and stared into the empty mug.

'I want to be a good mother to my son.'

'And?'

'And I want to build up my business

so that I can sell it and move on. That's all.'

'Sell it and move on?' he mused. 'No room for a man?'

'It would be nice to have a dad for Andy, but that is out of the question.'

'Why?'

Rosie would rather not say. She meant to tell him as little as possible.

'Well, it's a bit complicated. I have to keep moving, you see, and, well, a woman can hardly expect a husband to agree to that, can she?'

Josh's eyes widened incredulously.

'Let's get this straight. You're on the run?'

'Not exactly. Well, I suppose . . . if you like to put it that way.'

'Why?'

'I'd rather not say.'

'Are you in trouble with the law?'

'No,' she answered, but her denial was a little too hasty. 'At least . . . '

'At least?'

'Never mind.'

She was going to say, 'At least, not

yet.' And that was the way it was going to stay, providing Andy's father didn't tumble to the fact that he had a son. She'd promised Andy's mother she'd keep the baby's existence a secret. Andy's father, she'd been told, was thoroughly unscrupulous, and not above appearing at any moment to whisk his son away. If that happened, Rosie didn't think she could bear it.

Josh was looking so sceptical that Rosie burst out, 'I'm not in any trouble with the law, and I'm not going to say any more about the subject!'

Josh was too much of a gentleman to press her. Instead, he tried a different tack.

'You said you once lived in Pretoria. How long ago was that?'

'I said that?'

'Sure you did, the other evening.'

'Oh, yes, of course.'

Rosie felt the dismay in the pit of her stomach as she lifted wary eyes to his. Had she really divulged that fact? That wretched tongue of hers!

'It was a long time ago,' she confessed vaguely, 'six or seven years. I can't remember. I moved there after Rob, my husband, was killed.'

'Would you mind telling me his full name and rank?'

Rosie told him, thinking it could do no harm.

'You had lots of friends in Pretoria?'

'Well, yes. Mainly Forces wives. You know how it is.'

No need to tell him about Andy's mother, her ex-flatmate.

'Look, can we change the subject?' Rosie urged.

Josh's eyes narrowed thoughtfully. Rosie had a secret, something which brought the shadows to those dark eyes, and it concerned her time in Pretoria. He experienced a sudden deep desire to protect her from whatever it was which troubled her. In fact, he had never wanted a woman as much as he wanted Rosie. He knew with sudden clarity that he wanted to spend the rest of his life with her. He became brisk.

'Right, let's talk about those tyres. You'll have to inform the police. This is the third incident of harassment you've had from the same quarter.'

* * *

Kevin Petty screwed a length of plank into a vice and set about planing it while Paul White stood by, issuing officious instructions in a pompous voice. Kevin's father, Sam, was tucked away in the office with the see-through wall at the other end of the shed, going over the books.

'I done it last night, like I said I would,' Paul mentioned with a smirk.

Kevin stopped planing and stared.

'Set fire to the shop?'

'No, bubblehead. I slit the tyres.'

At this, both youths fell about laughing.

'Come on, Kev, it's time to knock off. Let's go and have a drink at the Mountain View.'

Kevin threw down his plane.

'OK. You and me'll have a little wager as to how long that Little Miss Snooty'll last out.'

'Yeah, 'specially when her dainty little nostrils start smellin' all that antique junk goin' up in smoke.'

They left the shed without saying goodbye to the boss, but Sam Petty was well aware of their departure all the same. He grinned as he thought about his little secret. He'd had the building wired years ago in order to listen in on the conversations of his employees. It kept him informed, and he, in turn, was able to keep one step ahead of them.

He shut his file and locked it inside the steel cabinet before reaching for the keys of his vehicle. He might even join the boys at the Mountain View, keeping well out of sight. It would be fun to observe their little shenanigans. His Kev, he reflected proudly, was a right smart one. A chip off the old block! Fancy thinking up all those ways to get the woman to push off.

Sam gave another grin as he climbed

into his truck and fired the engine. Naturally should anything go wrong with their little schemes, he'd deny all knowledge. Kevin and his friend would have to carry the can themselves. It wouldn't do the business any good if he were to be connected with something like arson, now, would it?

★ ★ ★

Josh sat in the bar of the Mountain View Hotel, happily putting names and faces to the voices he'd been monitoring over the past few weeks. The colonel would be arriving in the morning and would expect a good report, farce though it was.

Josh grinned. The old man would get more than a report. He'd get a letter of resignation as well. He'd spent the afternoon in long, hard thought, and come to the conclusion that he no longer wished to be a fighting man. A flying man he always would be, but his lust for combat had disappeared.

Colonel Jenkins arrived the following morning, punctual to the second. He sat in Josh's living-room, heard him out and fixed his young officer with one of his fierce glares.

'You have given this decision considerable thought, Major?'

'Yes, sir. I cannot return to my job. You and I both know that, sir.'

The old man sighed.

'Yes. I had thought you would be happy to take up another, shall we say, less demanding position on my staff, but I see that your mind is quite made up. What will you do now?'

'I haven't decided that yet, sir. I would like to continue flying to some degree, providing I'm fit enough.'

'You have no interest in farming? Your family owns vast tracts of land on the other side of these mountains, I believe.'

'No, sir. Farming has never been my interest. Besides, I have two brothers who perform admirably in that arena.'

'I see. Well, you must have some idea

of what you want to do?'

Josh considered for a moment. He thought of his new awareness of the natural world about him and of the many radio programmes and television discussion panels he'd listened to over the past few weeks.

'I'm considering some sort of career with wild life,' he admitted.

The colonel hid his surprise. Of all his staff, he'd never have credited Major McGregor with a love of nature.

'I see. Well, it just so happens that I may be able to help.'

He reached into his briefcase and pulled out a glossy publication.

'Take a look at the latest African Conservation Journal, Major. I have an interest in wild-life conservation myself, as you know. The wife and I always take our holidays within short distances of any nature reserves, hence our presence in the Drakensberg at this time. We've just visited the Royal Natal National Park.'

He indicated the magazine.

'I notice that there are a number of positions going with the National Parks Board. You may be interested in one of them.'

Josh thanked him, ushered the colonel to his car and gave a sharp salute.

'Goodbye, sir. I'll be in touch with your office concerning my resignation.'

The colonel climbed into his car and allowed himself a small smile.

'Your report was interesting, Major. Not quite up to the required standard, however.'

'No, sir,' Josh said, grinning. 'I take it you will not be requiring another?'

'Certainly not.'

The old man switched on the ignition.

'I shall be sorry to lose you. You had such talent. Good luck, my boy.'

Josh watched the car disappear and heaved a great sigh of relief. He'd burned his bridges and there was no going back. After such a momentous decision, it was strange that all he could think about at that moment was sharing it with an intriguing woman he would like to know a good deal better. He returned to the living-room, intent on discovering what that journal contained. But instead of leafing through it, he picked up the telephone.

'I should like to hire one of your vehicles,' he told the clerk at the car-hire company in the neighbouring town of Estcourt.

It was time to resume life as he'd once known it. If he was ever going to fly again, the first step would be to see if he could still drive a motor car. Besides, he needed a car in order to take Rosie out to dinner this evening.

Rosie was polishing her shop window during a quiet period, gloomily reflecting that she hadn't made a single sale that afternoon. In fact, the whole day had been rather quiet and she was feeling just a little bored.

By closing time, Rosie had counted her small takings at least five times. At this rate she'd never be able to meet all her financial commitments at the end of the month. She needed money in hand for those house sales in Estcourt, too. It wasn't as though she could ignore them because she was compelled to take advantage of every opportunity she could find. It was imperative to maintain a reasonable level of stock if she was to succeed.

Rosie glanced up as a shiny blue limousine stopped outside the shop. When she saw who it was behind the wheel, she did a double-take. Josh, noting her reaction, hid his mirth.

'Good afternoon, Rosie,' he greeted her as he came into the shop.

'You're able to drive a car again? That's wonderful!'

In spite of her problems Rosie was happy for him.

'I'm just about to shut up shop. Would you like a cup of coffee?'

She was immensely glad to see him, but rationalised it by telling herself it was only because the day had been so tedious.

Josh's grey eyes gleamed with satisfaction. He'd been hoping for just such an invitation.

'Thank you, Rosie.'

'I'll just lock up and then fetch Andy from the Mitchell's. I won't be long.'

'I'll do that,' Josh offered. 'Just give me the directions.'

Rosie looked up at him gratefully.

'It's in Hill Street, the next road up from this one, number six. I'll go and put the kettle on.'

Andy and Tommy were in the Mitchells' front garden, encouraging Tommy's dog to jump through a hoop. All three of them had high hopes of joining Boswell's Circus when it next came to town! They stopped and stared curiously at the unfamiliar car which drew up at the kerb. To their amazement a very large man climbed out and gave them a friendly wave.

'Hi, Andy. You ready to come home? I have a surprise for you.'

Tommy's mouth dropped open.

'Who's that?'

Andy's chest swelled to twice its normal size.

'That,' he said proudly, 'is my dad!'

He grabbed his shoes, yelled goodbye and ran through the gate. Once seated, he turned to Josh, his face alight.

'This is a cool car. Thanks for coming to fetch me. I like big cars with squashy seats that smell of leather.'

'My pleasure, Andy.'

Andy gazed at him thoughtfully.

'I didn't know a blind man could drive a car.'

'I'm not blind any more, Andy. My sight has returned.'

'Oh.'

Andy's curiosity on that score vanished, to be replaced by something far more pressing.

'What's the surprise, Major?'

'I'm taking you and your mother out to dinner, if she's agreeable, that is.'

'Mum'll say no, I know she will. She doesn't like you, you know. At least, I think she does like you but she pretends not to.'

A fact Josh had already worked out for himself!

The car turned into Rosie's driveway and came to a smooth halt behind hers. Josh climbed out rather stiffly and flexed his knee, thankful to find the leg still in one piece. He turned a bland face to the small boy who was regarding him so anxiously from the driveway.

'You'll have to work on her, Major,' he advised seriously, 'like, buy her some flowers, or something.'

Josh assumed his man-to-man voice.

'Oh, I intend to, Andy. All she needs is a little time.'

Time was something he had plenty of, Josh reflected as he mounted the stairs to the flat — time to devise a definite strategy to make Rosie fall in love with him. And being a military man, he knew how to plan.

8

'I'd like to take you and Andy out to dinner tonight, Rosie,' Josh told her when they joined her in the flat.

Rosie looked up from pouring the coffee, her eyes wide.

'Whatever for?'

'I thought we could celebrate the return of my eyesight.'

'Oh, right.'

She hardly sounded enthusiastic.

'Well?'

Ever practical, Rosie told him reasonably, 'Well, I haven't started dinner yet, so there's nothing to spoil, is there? That would be very nice, Major.'

'Josh,' he reminded her.

Rosie turned to Andy who was following the exchange avidly.

'Go and have your bath, Andy, and be quick about it, please. Wear clean jeans and your new shirt.'

For once Andy didn't argue. He raced off to the bathroom.

'Where will we dine?' Rosie asked. 'Will I need to dress up?'

Josh said easily, 'You look very nice as you are, Rosie. I thought we'd find a small inn somewhere quiet.'

Rosie looked relieved.

'It's just that I'm not used to . . . '

'Dating?' he said, his voice full of tenderness.

She blushed becomingly.

'This is hardly a date, is it? I meant, I'm not used to eating out. May I make a suggestion?'

'Certainly.'

'Could we dine at that new burger place in Estcourt? Andy has been begging me to take him there.'

Josh agreed, hiding his disappointment beneath perfect manners. Welcome, McGregor, he thought, to the world of small children!

Andy emerged from his bedroom with damp hair, wearing a pair of jeans and nothing else.

'Mum, I can't find my new shirt.'

Rosie sighed.

'It's in your top drawer, Andy. Take another look.'

As Andy sped off she turned to Josh with a remark about small boys, but stopped in mid-sentence. He was staring after Andy's departing back, looking completely stunned.

'Is anything wrong?' Rosie asked.

A mask slid over Josh's features.

'That birthmark on Andy's side,' he said casually. 'It's very unusual.'

She thought of the tiny red irregular shape just above her son's right hip.

'Yes, I suppose it is. We call it his butterfly. It sort of looks like one, doesn't it? Now, will you excuse me? I'll go and tidy myself.'

Josh stood politely as she left the room, then went to the window and stared unseeingly at the garden below. It was astounding that Rosie's son possessed an identical genetic characteristic which had been a feature of his own family for generations!

$\star$ $\star$ $\star$

Andy polished off his burger and French fries and assured his mother that he still had plenty of room for ice-cream, and a milkshake.

'Cool,' he sighed ecstatically when the last drop had been extracted through the straw. 'Sorry, Mum, for slurping.'

Rosie tried to look severe, and failed. It was wonderful to see her son so happy.

'Have you quite finished?'

Andy nodded. He wasn't about to forget to thank his benefactor for such a smashing meal, either.

'Thank you very much, Major,' he breathed, his eyes shining.

'It's a pleasure, Andy,' Josh replied gravely.

It really was a pleasure, he realised in some surprise. Andy was entertaining company and he was beginning to feel an incredible fondness for the child. There was almost a spiritual bond between them, one he couldn't quite define. For that matter, Andy could have been his own son.

While the adults finished their coffee, Andy, with his mother's permission, went to examine the children's play area adjacent to the dining-room, leaving the adults free to chat for a few moments.

'Rosie,' Josh began.

Despite his relaxed manner something in his tone alerted Rosie to the fact that he wasn't as composed as he appeared to be. She pushed her empty cup aside.

'Yes, Josh?'

He gave her a steady look.

'Would you tell me about Andy? He's such a charming child, I'd like to get to know him a lot better.'

'What exactly would you like to know?'

'Oh, things like, where he was born, and when? We might do something special on his next birthday.'

Rosie immediately relaxed, rattling

off her son's birth date.

'He was born in Pretoria, I presume?' Josh asked.

'Yes, of course.'

'Did you have an easy time?'

Rosie swallowed. She looked at him guiltily, saying quickly, 'It was a normal birth, yes.'

'I see.'

Josh studied his fingernails. Rosie was a rotten liar. Her nervousness had given him his answer quite clearly — she was not Andy's birth mother, he was certain. Another piece of the puzzle fell into place for Josh. It explained her behaviour on a number of occasions, and he found himself more than ever determined to unravel her little secret, especially now that he'd discovered the McGregor butterfly on Andy's body. His brother had lived in Pretoria for a while, and he'd had a reputation with the ladies. Could he possibly be Andy's real father? It became imperative all at once to discover the identity of the biological mother, too.

They collected Andy from the play area and drove back to Rosie's flat where Andy took himself to bed in the happiest of moods. His dad was really, really cool, he told his green rubber snake before placing it lovingly under his pillow.

Josh declined Rosie's offer of another cup of coffee, listened gravely to her little speech of thanks then did something he'd been waiting to do all evening. He bent to kiss her, an unhurried kiss which left her quite breathless. She gazed up at him, her cheeks pink, her eyes telling him so much more than she realised, so that Josh was moved to tighten his arms about her and repeat the performance. He was delighted to discover that Rosie's response was all that he could have hoped for.

'Good-night, Rosie, sleep well,' he told her, and disappeared quickly down the steps.

Rosie stood gazing after him into the darkness, shocked at the depth of feeling his kisses had aroused in her. Not that she should be surprised. Hadn't she already fallen madly in love with him? If the truth be told, the very first time she'd looked into those stunning grey eyes she'd made the momentous discovery that Major Josh McGregor was the only man she would ever consider marrying, if she were even remotely interested in the marriage stakes again — which she wasn't!

With a sigh of regret she took herself to bed.

Next morning, Josh took Dan for his usual walk, cooked himself a large breakfast and settled down to plan his strategy with military precision. He had fallen in love with Rosie Carlisle and her son, and wanted nothing better than to turn them into a proper family, despite the mystery which Rosie appeared to be guarding so fiercely.

He set about making careful plans. First, he needed to find himself a job. Second, he needed to give Rosie both time and opportunity to fall in love with him, if he could wait that long, that is. Third, he needed to make some phone calls concerning Andy.

By the end of the morning, he was smiling. The colonel had already paved the way for him, it seemed. The National Parks Board was indeed looking for a pilot who would be prepared to taxi their veterinarians into the country's vast and numerous game parks every week, preferably someone with a real interest in wild life, and someone who would be prepared to understudy the game rangers with the view to providing vacation cover if necessary. All was exactly just up Josh's street.

Not that he needed to work at all, for his late father had left him a sizeable inheritance which had been wisely invested. However, Josh was not a man to live the life of a playboy. He needed a challenge. This new direction would provide just that. It was with real pleasure that he anticipated the interview which had been arranged for him the following day.

He'd also telephoned the florist in Estcourt and ordered a large bouquet of roses to be delivered to Rosie's shop that afternoon, together with a note thanking her and Andy for a pleasant evening. Andy would be impressed, he thought with a grin. Then he had one more call to make before lunch.

Josh picked up the telephone and dialled long-distance to a friend who worked in the office of the Registrar of Births and Deaths, in Pretoria.

'Charles? It's Josh McGregor. I need a favour.'

Charles Reynolds thought about the way in which Major McGregor had once saved his life during a sky-diving exercise they had both been involved in, and immediately acquiesced.

'Anything, Josh. What can I do for you?'

'I need copies of some certificates . . . the death certificate of a certain Robert John Carlisle, killed on active service in Angola.' Having an excellent memory he was able to cite the man's rank and regiment, adding, 'You may even find something in the Army archives.'

'No problem. Leave it to me. And the other?'

'I want the full birth certificate of an Andrew John Carlisle.'

He gave Andy's date and place of birth.

'Let me know what the cost is, Charles, and I'll send you a cheque. Kindly forward the certificates as soon as possible to this address.'

He cited a box number at the Winterberg post office, thanked his friend warmly and rang off.

'Well, Dan,' he informed the Labrador as he set about heating up the remains of yesterday's stew, 'things are moving. By this time next week, we'll have cracked Rosie's little secret!'

* * *

Etta de Wit was agog. She'd been standing in her front garden inspecting her autumn flowering chrysanthemums when a shiny blue limousine had driven past. It wasn't the car which worried her, though, it was the driver. He'd looked extraordinarily like that man with the Labrador, the one with the red cap and the white stick, who lived near the dam.

'And what, may I ask, was a blind man doing, racing around in a fancy car?' she demanded of her friend, Mrs Morgan, the following afternoon as they drank tea in the lounge of the Mountain View Hotel in Winterberg. 'I told you he wasn't what he seemed, Maggie. The man's up to no good.'

'Oh, I don't know, Etta,' her friend objected. 'The man seems perfectly respectable to me. He even sent flowers to that nice Rosie Carlisle yesterday. I was in the shop when they arrived. She was very flustered about it all, too, blushing like a bride. It's my belief that she's half in love with him. Not that I blame her, mind you. He's incredibly handsome, isn't he?'

Mrs de Wit huffed.

'The fact he's sniffing round Rosie Carlisle proves he's up to something. What decent man would involve himself with a girl like her?'

'What do you mean, Etta?'

'She's not what she seems, I tell you. I know it because my son, George, was in the army with her late husband, Captain Robert Carlisle.'

'What does that prove, Etta?'

Mrs de Wit sniffed.

'Captain Carlisle died eight and a half years ago. I know it because he should have been discharged at the same time as my George. They were in the same regiment, but he was killed in action the week before.'

'So?'

'Well, don't you see? That son of hers, Andy, is only six. You told me so yourself. He couldn't possibly be her husband's child now, could he?'

She broke off in consternation as the object of their discussion appeared unexpectedly from the kitchen regions of the hotel wearing a black skirt, white blouse and frilly apron.

'Good gracious, Maggie, here she comes,' Etta gasped.

Rosie approached the table with a smile.

'Good afternoon, ladies. Your waitress has now gone off duty. Can I get you anything else?'

Mrs de Wit found her voice admirably.

'Oh, hello, dear,' she squeaked. 'No, nothing else, thank you, just bring us the bill,' she went on then, unable to restrain her curiosity, she demanded, 'What are you doing here?'

'I'm helping out,' Rosie explained, reflecting that it was better to tell the two old biddies exactly what the story was before they began making it up for themselves.

'But your shop?'

'I closed it for the afternoon because

Lucy and Daniel asked me to hold the fort here. Daniel's taken Lucy into the hospital in Estcourt. She has gone into labour.'

9

It was a few afternoons later that Josh decided to walk into the village rather than take the car. He considered it high time for some exercise for both himself and Dan, and besides, he needed to collect his post.

He arrived at the post office, extracted a key from the pocket of his jeans and opened his mail box, unconscious of the peculiar stares he was receiving from the other customers. Rumours, courtesy of Mrs de Wit, had been rife all week in the village of Winterberg!

Josh extracted the letters, discarded one or two items of junk mail and gave the postmistress a polite nod before heading in the direction of the Mountain View Hotel where he determined to buy himself a cup of coffee and read his mail in peace. He chose his usual seat on the terrace and began to slit open an envelope.

Daniel Allbright, all smiles, delivered the tray together with the news that his wife, Lucy, had recently been delivered of a healthy son.

'That's wonderful,' Josh enthused, really meaning it. 'Please offer Lucy my warmest congratulations. You're a lucky man, Allbright.'

'Don't I know it, Major!'

'The name is Josh.'

After all, he intended to become part of Rosie's family in the near future!

'May I call you Daniel?'

The two men chatted amiably for a few minutes before Daniel returned to the kitchen. Josh immediately retrieved the envelope he had been trying to open. On the back was the stamp of the Registrar of Births and Deaths. Good old Charles had come through for him!

As Josh read the contents, the blood drained from his face. A few minutes later he quietly left the hotel, his coffee untouched.

Daniel, coming to collect the tray a while later, shook his head in bewilderment. Odd chap, Major McGregor . . .

That night, a silver moon shone seductively through Rosie's window, bathing her bed in silver, unperturbed by the furtive activities of the two young men in the street below.

Rosie awakened some time during the night, wondering what had roused her. It was a sort of hissing noise, together with a foul smell. When she realised what it was, she flung back the covers and raced into Andy's room, her heart beating crazily. He was asleep, curled up in his usual position, quite oblivious that their lives were in danger.

Rosie shot back into the passage to find that the internal door to the shop was already crackling with heat. Nasty, acrid smoke was billowing underneath it, spewing fumes into the tiny hallway. Her shop was on fire!

Grabbing the telephone, Rosie dialled 999 before running back to her bedroom. She pulled on a pair of jeans and a sweater, and thrust her feet into the first pair of shoes she could find. Then she ran to rouse Andy. In a calm voice she urged the sleepy boy into his shoes and dressing-gown, thrust a wet facecloth over his mouth and nose and hustled him through the smoke to the front door. As they reached it, the living-room floor gave way, crashing into the room below with a fearful noise.

Rosie remembered to grab her car keys from the hall table, thankful that she and Andy were at least able to escape down the concrete stairway on the outside of the building. The night was already split by the sound of sirens as both police and firemen arrived at the same time.

Rosie stood clutching Andy on the pavement, overwhelmed by an icy despair. Everything she and Andy owned in the whole wide world was going up in smoke.

A few hours later, safely ensconced in one of the bedrooms at the Mountain

View Hotel, Rosie allowed herself the luxury of a good weep. She'd even lost Andy's birth certificate, everything.

It wasn't long before the light of dawn crept into her bedroom and Rosie, an early riser by habit, washed her face, made free with Lucy's toiletries and brushed her hair into some semblance of order before going down to breakfast. Andy, still in his pyjamas, was pale and tired, but nevertheless filled with suppressed excitement.

'Wait until I tell Tommy,' he babbled as he tucked into a bowl of cereal.

Tommy's mother, Jean Mitchell, arrived after breakfast with a pile of clothing over one arm.

'I thought Andy would like to go to school,' she offered tentatively. 'He can wear these. I'll take him now with Tommy, if you like. You're bound to be busy today with police statements, insurance people, and the like.'

Rosie, touched at the gesture, thanked her sincerely, but hadn't the heart to mention that she'd had no insurance whatever. She then took her cup of coffee out on to the terrace, hoping a breath of fresh air would stimulate her tired brain. She needed to formulate some plan of action, and quickly.

Perhaps she could leave Andy with Lucy for a few days and drive into Estcourt or any of the other larger towns, to look for work. The sooner she found a job, the sooner they could move on and begin again. It was the story of their lives, she thought wearily.

Lucy, spying her sister through the dining-room window, came out to the terrace, carrying her small son. She darted Rosie a look of sisterly concern.

'I'm so sorry this had to happen to you, love. What will you do now? You can stay here for as long as you need, you know.'

'Thanks, but I must move on, Lucy, as usual! Things aren't safe here.'

'Are you sure?'

'Yes, but I can tell you, I'm getting

heartily sick of it. If only I knew for sure what Andy's father was really like. I only have his ex-wife's word for it, you know. Perhaps the man isn't quite the ogre she made him out to be. Perhaps he's remarried and has other children, and might not be at all interested to hear that he has another son, or maybe he simply wouldn't want to be lumbered with another child. Perhaps he'd let me keep Andy.'

'Oh, he'd let you keep Andy all right,' Josh's voice came quietly from behind them. 'It's my guess that he might even ask you to marry him.'

Rosie dropped her empty cup into its saucer with a clatter.

'I beg your pardon?' she gasped.

Josh regarded her inscrutably.

'Well, it's what I would do, anyway. I'd marry the woman.'

He turned to Lucy.

'I'd like to speak to Rosie privately, if I may.'

Lucy, agog with curiosity, jumped up.

'Of course. Shall I order you a cup of coffee?'

Josh gave her a warm smile.

'That would be nice. Bring your sister another one, too. She looks as though she needs it.'

Rosie's large eyes were darker than ever. Josh cleared his throat.

'Rosie.'

She had never heard that note in his voice before, tenderness mixed with uncertainty.

'Yes?'

'Rosie, will you marry me?'

Her pretty mouth fell open and her pansy dark eyes held complete bewilderment. This, on top of the trauma she'd just experienced, was too much! She burst into tears. Calmly Josh handed her his handkerchief.

'I love you, Rosie,' he told her. 'Will you marry me?'

Rosie managed an unladylike hiccough.

'In case you don't know it, I have just had a most harrowing and distressing few hours, so I'm bound to be a little slow-witted this morning. I could be in a state of shock, still, but did you just propose marriage?'

Josh gazed at her, his heart in his eyes.

'I certainly did.'

'But why?'

'I'll tell you. I have loved you ever since you tried to kill me on the road to Winterberg! I loved your voice, your sassy independence. Then when I saw you in the flesh I was enchanted, completely and utterly smitten. I wanted you for myself. I wanted to know you better, but you had a secret, Rosie, which kept you away from me. I determined to discover what it was.'

He paused.

'I know all about Andy.'

At her look of horror, he reached for her hands.

'I know who Andy's mother is,' then corrected himself, 'Who she was.'

'Was?'

'Lucinda was killed in a boating

accident when Andy was only a few months old, along with her new husband.'

'How do you know all this?' Rosie croaked.

'Lucinda was my wife.'

Rosie could only stare.

'Andy must have been conceived just before Lucinda left me,' Josh informed her gently. 'She didn't tell me about the pregnancy even though to my knowledge she never wanted a child. But to her eternal credit, she didn't get rid of the baby.'

'Lucinda McGregor,' Rosie whispered, 'was your wife? She never once mentioned your name or I would have recognised it when I met you.'

She wiped the tears from her face and continued.

'For some months before Andy was born, I shared my flat with her. I was lonely and she said she needed a place to stay until she could give birth. When the baby arrived, she just didn't want anything to do with it, or her

179

family. She begged me to take him so that she could begin a new life with the man she really wanted, an American airman, I believe. Before she left for the States, she informed me that Andy's real father was a monster and didn't deserve to know that he had a son.'

Josh winced.

'That sounds like Lucinda.'

Rosie shook her head as if to clear it.

'So what you're really saying is that now that you've found your son, you want him back. Can you prove Andy is your son?'

'I've checked the dates, and they tally.'

'How do you know that Lucinda didn't . . . that Andy is really yours?'

Josh pulled his shirt from his trousers.

'He has the McGregor butterfly,' he told her, and revealed his own.

Rosie stared. To one side of Josh's flat, tanned abdomen she saw it, a small, irregular mark.

'My grandfather had it and his father

before him,' Josh explained. 'When I noticed Andy's mark the other day, I had my suspicions. I thought maybe you'd had an affair with my brother, but I was convinced you had never borne a child, so you couldn't be Andy's mother. That was when I decided to obtain a copy of his birth certificate.'

Josh pulled a document from his pocket.

'It cites Lucinda's name but omits mine, for obvious reasons. She had no intention that I should ever find out.'

Rosie had caught sight of another document underneath.

'What's that?'

'Your late husband's death certificate. I had to be sure that he couldn't possibly have fathered Andy, not that I ever seriously thought he had.'

Rosie lifted pansy dark eyes to his. She felt nothing but immense relief that her secret was out in the open at last.

'Would you want to have a paternity test?'

'No need.'

'Then where do we go from here?'

Josh waited patiently as a waitress appeared and placed a tray of coffee on the table. Then with military precision, he told her.

'First, we go down to the village and take another look at the scene of the fire, to see if there is anything which can be salvaged. Second, we inform the police of our suspicions of arson. I am sure if they look hard enough they'll find the source. Third, we collect Andy from school and tell him that we are to be married as soon as possible. Fourth, we buy the two of you some new clothing.'

'Just a moment,' Rosie interrupted. 'Why the rush? You're taking a lot for granted, Joshua McGregor. I haven't even agreed to marry you yet.'

'I am not a patient man, Rosie. I like to get things done. I have a new job to go to, with a large house in one of the country's most prestigious nature reserves. There will be every species of frog imaginable, not to mention a thousand other life forms. Andy will have a field day. And, the house is very old. I saw it the other day. The living-room fireplace has a Victorian, ceramic surround. I can just see a gilded French bergère or a painted English Chippendale-style armchair alongside it. In fact, you can fill the whole darned place with Victoriana if you so wish.'

Rosie's mouth had fallen open.

'How do you know all that about antiques?'

He ignored her.

'I have to start work in two weeks' time, Rosie,' he pointed out reasonably, 'and you'll want to get there as soon as possible to measure up for all those new curtains.'

'Put like that,' Rosie grumbled, 'how can I refuse? There's just one other question. Why would you want to marry a girl who doesn't love you?'

'You're a poor liar, Rosie. Of course you love me,' Josh informed her.

A small smile played about Rosie's mouth.

'Well, maybe just a little. And I like the sound of that fireplace.'

'That's settled then. You'll marry me?'

'Well, yes.'

She'd never really been in any doubt!

Josh's patience had all but exhausted itself. He stood up, tucked his shirt back into his trousers and opened his arms.

'Then come here, my reluctant, little darling.'

A few moments later, Daniel Allbright bustled out to the terrace to fetch the empty tray. His jaw dropped at the sight of his sister-in-law being thoroughly kissed by a very large airman who looked about to take off and fly them both into the blue yonder!

With a smothered grin he made a hasty retreat to the kitchen to report matters to his wife and baby son.

Major Josh McGregor's coffee, yet again, had remained untouched . . .

We do hope that you have enjoyed reading this large print book.

Did you know that all of our titles are available for purchase?

We publish a wide range of high quality large print books including:
Romances, Mysteries, Classics
General Fiction
Non Fiction and Westerns

Special interest titles available in large print are:
The Little Oxford Dictionary
Music Book, Song Book
Hymn Book, Service Book

Also available from us courtesy of Oxford University Press:
Young Readers' Dictionary
(large print edition)
Young Readers' Thesaurus
(large print edition)

For further information or a free brochure, please contact us at:
Ulverscroft Large Print Books Ltd.,
The Green, Bradgate Road, Anstey,
Leicester, LE7 7FU, England.
Tel: (00 44) **0116 236 4325**
Fax: (00 44) **0116 234 0205**

THREE TALL TAMARISKS

Christine Briscomb

Joanna Baxter flies from Sydney to run her parents' small farm in the Adelaide Hills while they recover from a road accident. But after crossing swords with Riley Kemp, life is anything but uneventful. Gradually she discovers that Riley's passionate nature and quirky sense of humour are capturing her emotions, but a magical day spent with him on the coast comes to an abrupt end when the elegant Greta intervenes. Did Riley love Greta after all?